All that mattered was Isla and Mazi.

"Adan, stop." She dragged her overnight bag off the couch. It thudded hard against her leg, but Isla wouldn't ever admit if it had hurt. "You've already taken a bullet for me. Almost two. You saved my life out there in the desert, and you look like you're on the verge of collapse. At some point you're going to have to stop sacrificing your needs for us. Let this be a first step. All right? Take the bigger bed."

She didn't wait for him to argue, heading down the hallway toward Mazi's room.

Even with the burn of her instructions fresh, a big part of him liked their back-and-forth. Low voices filtered down the hall from the back room. He wasn't alone. For the first time since he'd left the military, he had someone to take care of, to talk to, to laugh with.

Hard to do with a bullet wound in his shoulder, but he could do it.

OVER HER DEAD BODY

Nichole Severn

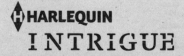

To all of you!

Thank you for believing in this series.

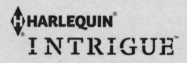

ISBN-13: 978-1-335-58260-7

Over Her Dead Body

Copyright © 2023 by Natascha Jaffa

Recycling programs
for this product may
not exist in your area.

For questions and comments about the quality of this book,
please contact us at CustomerService@Harlequin.com.

Harlequin Enterprises ULC
22 Adelaide St. West, 41st Floor
Toronto, Ontario M5H 4E3, Canada
www.Harlequin.com

Printed in U.S.A.

Nichole Severn writes explosive romantic suspense with strong heroines, heroes who dare challenge them and a hell of a lot of guns. She resides with her very supportive and patient husband, as well as her demon spawn, in Utah. When she's not writing, she's constantly injuring herself running, rock climbing, practicing yoga and snowboarding. She loves hearing from readers through her website, www.nicholesevern.com, and on Facebook, @nicholesevern.

Books by Nichole Severn

Harlequin Intrigue

Defenders of Battle Mountain

Grave Danger
Dead Giveaway
Dead on Arrival
Presumed Dead
Over Her Dead Body

A Marshal Law Novel

The Fugitive
The Witness
The Prosecutor
The Suspect

Blackhawk Security

Rules in Blackmail
Rules in Rescue
Rules in Deceit
Rules in Defiance
Caught in the Crossfire
The Line of Duty

Visit the Author Profile page at Harlequin.com.

CAST OF CHARACTERS

Isla Vachs—This single mother became a Battle Mountain reserve officer to learn to protect her family, but when a shooter opens fire in the middle of town, she's suddenly confronted by her greatest nightmare: her daughter becoming an orphan.

Adan Sergeant—It's his duty to protect his deceased best friend's wife and daughter. Overseeing Isla and her daughter's safety is his only priority, but the closer they get, the more dangerous his assignment becomes.

Weston Ford—Chief Ford is at the public's mercy. With his department under scrutiny from Battle Mountain government and its citizens, he's not sure he can help stop this new threat.

Macie Barclay—Battle Mountain PD's dispatcher is used to sitting behind a desk, but this time she'll have to break all the rules to make sure this town and the department survive a rogue sniper.

Chapter One

A small town didn't run on a twenty-four-hour news cycle. A small town never forgot.

"But how are you going to keep us safe?" The stranger's voice drowned the low murmurings filtering in and out.

Reserve Officer Isla Vachs leaned against one wall at the back of the room. It was a new career. And her decision to take it had been born in fear and blood and desperation. Just like this meeting. For one night, the basketball court of Battle Mountain's rec center had been transformed into an impromptu town hall. Nearly two hundred people scooted in metal chairs, raised questions and talked over one another.

They hadn't gotten anywhere the past hour.

"I give you my word as your police chief, Battle Mountain PD is doing everything in our power to keep you safe." Chief Weston Ford gripped the podium a bit too tight at the head of the assembly. But nothing he said—no number of promises—would give these people comfort. Their small former mining town was on the brink of destruction. Two serial killers, a bomber who'd taken a chunk out of Main Street to cover up a murder, and just a couple months ago, a man running from his past and leaving bodies in his wake.

This town had already lost so much. They all had.

They couldn't risk losing their faith, too.

"What is your word worth?" A woman in the center of the mass stood up, a toddler on one hip. Isla didn't know her name. "You only stepped into this job after Charlie Frasier couldn't do it anymore. What qualifies you to run a police department?"

Isla's gaze cut to the line of reserve officers off to her right, officers she should be standing with. She hadn't known any of them long, but what she did know of them made up for the confusion and doubt spreading through the room. Easton Ford—Weston's brother; Alma Majors, Battle Mountain's first female officer; Kendric Hudson, who was a former ATF instructor. Cree Gregson was a transplant, same as Kendric, from Larimer County's bomb squad. The men and women of this department had risked their lives and the lives of their loved ones to keep this town safe. But their expressions said it all: this meeting was just the beginning of the department's downfall.

"I understand your concerns. I've heard them." Townspeople quieted a moment as the chief leveled his gaze on them from one end of the room to the other. "And with the recent shooting of one of our EMTs, the department is recruiting more officers."

Her side ached at the mere mention of the bullet she'd taken through and through outside her own fire station two months ago. No new leads. No ballistics or witness statements. All she had to show for it was a still-healing wound and a memory of someone being there that night. Someone she couldn't remember.

The chief continued. "We're running more patrols. Both Silverton and Ouray are lending—"

"It's not enough!" came another voice.

Citizens clapped and nodded in an uproar, and Isla couldn't help but agree. This town had turned into a hub for criminals and fugitives alike. Once a tourist destination for its lakes, hiking trails and quiet escape, Battle Mountain had dried into something unrecognizable. They'd gotten all the publicity this past year, but for the wrong reasons. Without mining money keeping people employed or tourists adding to the economy, this place would cease to exist. It was only a matter of time.

"What about the investigation from the state?" another called.

Mayor Wayne Higgins shouldered the chief out of the way. A familiar figure with his limp and oversize cane, he seemed to have been Battle Mountain's chief executive ever since the town was founded. Raising both hands, he quieted down the panicked murmurs spreading across the lacquered floor. "Now, listen here. You have every right to be concerned. The past year has been hard on us all, but Chief Ford isn't placating you with fantasies. These are real, actionable steps we're taking to ensure you and your families are safe." He motioned to two women a little down the wall from Isla. "Our very own coroner, Dr. Chloe Miles, and District Attorney Alexander are living examples of the risk the men and women of this police department are willing to take for any one of us. Not to mention all those who were impacted by the bombing on Main Street or the forest fire set six months ago. Chief Ford and his officers have been there to battle our demons for us, and we owe him and his officers our respect and gratitude."

The room went silent.

Warning pooled at the base of Isla's spine.

Like the mayor had been building up to something with that little speech.

He paused, his hard gaze diverting to Chief Ford for a moment, before facing his voters again. "As for the internal affairs investigation from the Colorado Bureau of Investigations, there was nothing for Officer Dwyer to report. However, considering her personal involvement with one of the reserve officers and to make sure that we have the right people looking out for us, I will be conducting my own investigation into Battle Mountain PD."

Hoots and agreement burst from the audience.

Another round of clapping drowned out the mayor's next words.

Isla straightened from the wall, aggravating the hole in her side, as Chief Ford covered the microphone to have a sidebar with the mayor. Her fellow officers looked from one to another. Their confusion pierced through her. What did that mean? What kind of investigation? She'd moved from fire and rescue into the police department to ensure she could protect herself and her daughter, Mazi, in case the shooter tried a second time, but as the department's newest recruit, wouldn't she be the first to go if the mayor decided to clean house?

The chief seemingly gave up trying to get his own answers and stalked off the stage toward his officers, that recognizable ten-gallon hat in hand. Dr. Chloe Miles pushed through the throng to get to her husband, their three-month-old infant strapped to her chest. The district attorney, Genevieve Alexander, followed in her wake, wheeling through the audience.

Nervous energy solidified in Isla's veins as she walked to join her colleagues.

"The mayor is out of his damn mind." Cree Gregson crossed his arms over his muscled chest. "Campbell didn't find anything. Neither will he."

"It's not the investigation I'm worried about." Chief Ford nodded toward the townspeople. "It's them. If they have any doubts about us, they won't rely on us to help. So we cooperate. Whatever the mayor has in mind, you go along with it for however long it takes. Understand? These people need us." His gaze landed on Isla. "And they deserve to have someone standing up for them."

"I'll talk to Campbell, see if there's anything she can do to hurry this along. I'm sure she still has her files from the investigation she ran for CBI." Kendric Hudson pulled his phone from his pocket. "But something tells me Mayor Higgins wouldn't take the help."

"It's a start." The chief nodded. "Now get back to patrol."

Her fellow officers dispersed, each with their partner in tow. Except for the chief. He smoothed his hand over the baby's back and kissed Chloe lightly. Isla turned from the personal show of affection, her heart in her throat. Too familiar. Too painful.

A hard knock into her shoulder suctioned the air from her lungs as the townspeople filed out. No apologies followed after. It had been a deliberate strike to show BMPD officers they weren't up to par. What had she just walked into?

"Vachs." The chief's heavy footsteps closed in. She turned to face him, noting Chloe helping the district attorney and her wheelchair out a side door. "You're probably wondering what you've gotten yourself involved in. If you made the right move from fire and rescue."

From the limited interactions she'd had with Weston

Ford since coming to Battle Mountain, she'd learned he was the kind of man who'd rather deal straight than have anything sugarcoated. "Something along those lines, but I'm here now. There's no going back. Have you heard anything from the lab?"

His gaze deflected to the last few residents filing out the door past them, and the chief lowered his voice. "The bullet they pulled from you isn't connected to any other crimes in the database. Whoever pulled the trigger most likely made sure the gun was clean."

Her gut clenched just a bit. Hard to imagine why someone would've targeted her in the first place. She was a single mother of an eight-year-old spitfire, widowed and in the business of saving lives. Which meant the shooting had probably been random, and made it even more impossible to narrow down a motive or a suspect.

She cleared her throat to counter the terrifying memories of that night, of not knowing if Mazi was going to become an orphan. The girl had already lost her father. She couldn't lose her mother, too.

Isla hiked her thumbs into her belt. "Any other leads?"

"No." Genuine regret etched into the chief's expression. The weight of keeping this entire town safe had fallen on his shoulders the past few years, and it was starting to show. Not as quick to respond to his brother's barbs, slower to smile at Dr. Miles. And now he had to face an investigation. "I know you want answers. We all do. Even when you were with fire and rescue, you were one of us, and we won't stop until we figure out who shot you. I've got everyone keeping an eye out. We hear something, you'll be the first to know. Until then, be safe out there."

"Thanks, Chief." She didn't know what else to say. As much as she wanted to believe her new boss meant what he'd said—that she wasn't alone in this—Isla couldn't dislodge the need to find the truth on her own. She nodded goodbye, then headed out the door into the cooling night.

Fall was on the cusp. Dead leaves blew across the parking lot, triggering her awareness so high that she felt as though she'd jump right out of her own skin. The parking lot had cleared. Her oversize pickup truck waited in the back. Not hers. Clint's. It had been his pride and joy before he died.

Battle Mountain PD was actively recruiting officers, but resources didn't grow on trees. She had to use her personal vehicle. All ten miles to the gallon of it. Thankfully, the town wasn't that big, and she only had between two or three shifts a week.

Isla unpocketed her keys and disengaged the top-of-the-line alarm. Clint had decked it out a few months before his last tour. As much as she hated hauling herself and Mazi into the monster, she couldn't convince herself to sell it for something more practical. It had been the last project he'd worked on.

She slowed. The headlights hadn't flashed when she'd hit the button to unlock the truck. Crap. She wasn't tall enough to reach the engine to check the battery without help. Frustration bubbled up her throat. She really needed to get rid of the truck. Sliding her phone from her slacks, she scrolled to Easton Ford's name to call for an assist. He was tall enough to reach under the hood. And if he wasn't, she'd have to wait until the auto parts store opened in the morning. There went her shift. "Damn it."

She hit dial and brought the phone to her ear.

An all-too-familiar crack of a bullet pierced through the night.

A split second before pain and a solid wall of muscle tackled her to the asphalt.

SHE'D BEEN HIT.

Adan Scrgcant shovcd himsclf off Isla's small frame. He fisted her uniform in both hands and dragged her behind the only vehicle left in the parking lot. Clint's. The monster truck would give them some cover, but the most pressing issue was his best friend's wife taking another bullet. He tugged her against the humongous tire of the front passenger side and patted her from shoulder to thigh to get a sense of her injuries. No blood. Hope exploded through his system. "Isla, can you hear me? Where are you hit?"

A wild confusion and a drastic amount of pain infiltrated her normally emotionless expression. She pressed her heels into the asphalt and ripped at her shirt collar. Parking lot lights glinted off the shiny butt of a bullet lodged in the center of her chest. She struggled around her next breath. "Vest."

"Good girl." His gun was already in hand. He shoved to stand. She'd live. That was all that mattered. But two bullets in as few as two months was challenging her luck. He might not be there if the shooter came after Isla a third time.

He needed to end this now.

Darkness shifted with strong winds ripping through the trees. They were at a disadvantage here. Targets. The shooter had chosen the perfect position to take the shot. No movement. No sign of the gunman at all. Adan's heart pounded hard behind his ears. This was just like Morocco. Too many variables. Not enough intel.

"Southeast. The bullet came from the southeast." A groan escaped up Isla's delicate throat. She pressed one hand into her chest and withdrew her sidearm with the other as she stood. Ready to face whatever waited for them on the other side of the truck. "I'm guessing he took position in those trees."

Isla reached for the radio at her belt. In seconds, she'd hailed the rest of the reserve officers in her department.

She'd already taken one bullet when he'd been too late to tackle her out of the way mere weeks ago. He wasn't going to fail her again. He wasn't going to fail Clint. Adan ducked, keeping the truck between him and the shooter. If he could work his way behind the bastard, he might have a shot of getting Isla out of here alive. "Cover me."

"You seem to have it a bit backward here. I'm Battle Mountain police, and you—" The weight of Isla's attention pressurized the air lodged in his chest. One second. Two. Every cell in his body feared and hoped for her to recognize him in an instant. Her outline seemed to harden right in front of him as though every muscle she owned had tensed in defense. With good reason. "Adan?"

"Hey, Bugs." The nickname he'd called her all those years ago wouldn't help things, but it was hard to break old habits.

"What are you…?" She didn't move, didn't even seem to breathe. It wasn't until Isla stepped forward that he got a good look at her up close. She'd cut her mass of dark brown waves short. Just below her ears. She was somehow leaner than before. Then again, it had been close to a year since he'd seen her last. Up close, anyway. Still just as beautiful, but the light she'd somehow emanated from within had burnt out. He could see it in her eyes. All that was left was pain. Because of him. "You've got a lot of guts showing up here—"

Another shot punched through the night.

Glass rained down around them. Isla ducked her

head with a sharp scream, but it wouldn't be enough to stop a bullet from coming through the truck and finding its target.

"And here I thought saving you from dying a second time would earn me a thank-you." Adan maneuvered around her and balanced his weapon across the truck hood. He pulled the trigger. Once. Twice. His instincts said he hadn't hit anything significant—no shooters falling out of trees—but it would distract the bastard long enough to give them a chance to run. "Come on. We're too vulnerable here. We need to get you somewhere safe."

Adan gripped the underside of her elbow.

She ripped free of his hold. "You're out of your damn mind if you think I'm going anywhere with you—"

Sirens pierced through the night. Isla turned toward the bright red and blue patrol lights with a wince of pain. She blocked her face with the raise of her free hand, but Adan made sure she stayed behind the truck. Anyone willing to take a shot at one police officer wouldn't hesitate to bring down three.

"BMPD! Drop the weapon! Get on the ground! Now!" Two uniformed officers raced to the hood of the car and took aim. At Adan.

"It's okay. I'm a friend." Hell. They were going to take him in. They were going to leave Isla unprotected while they wasted time processing him and checking out his story. Adan scanned the trees where the bullet had originated. Shadows shifted. Or was his desperation to protect Isla creating something that wasn't really there? Either way, this wasn't over. He could feel it, but what other choice did he have here but to do as BMPD ordered?

Turning back, he followed instructions and tossed his gun. For Isla's sake. The quicker the police cleared him, the sooner he could get her and Mazi out of Dodge. Metal thudded hard against asphalt—too loud in his ears—as his adrenaline from the shooting drained. His heart rate leveled off, and Adan dropped to his knees. Then onto his chest.

Isla backed away, the full brilliance of her face visible in the headlights.

"You good, Vachs?" One of the officers closed in, weapon steady. The man's deep voice resonated with a protectiveness that only came from being responsible for a unit under his care.

She dislodged the bullet from her vest, slightly bent over as though trying to catch her breath. She handed it off just as the second officer extended a clear plastic bag. The bullet hit the bottom and was sealed as evidence. Isla sagged against the tire of her husband's truck but managed to stay on her feet. That alone was a testament to her strength, but her decision to put herself in harm's way had already triggered consequences. "Good? No. Someone just took another shot at me, and I think he knows why."

Cuffs ratcheted around Adan's wrists at the small

of his back. The officer hauled him to his feet, but Adan only had attention for Isla.

"You know this guy?" The sliver of a name tag reflected the patrol car's headlights. Ford. But not the chief of police. No. This one was the former Green Beret. That information should've dosed him with a shot of relief. The man had combat experience. Easton Ford had honed a specific set of skills to stay alive and protect those in his unit, to guard the men and women in the department. Just like Adan. But the relief never came. It wasn't Easton Ford's duty to protect Isla. It was Adan's.

"Doesn't matter right now. He's not the one who took a shot at me. The shooter was positioned in those trees." She nodded toward the wall of black separating the parking lot from the rest of town. This was the perfect location to get the drop on her. "He'll be long gone by now."

Her confidence lined up with Adan's. As much as he feared the sniper would take out as many officers as he could, the shooter wouldn't want to risk getting into a shootout with the police until his assignment was complete. It would only draw attention. Both times the son of a bitch had gunned for Isla, he'd pulled the trigger from the dark. But that didn't mean she was safe during the day, either.

"Alma, stay with our new friend here and let Weston know we're bringing him in." Ford was already shoving Adan toward the female officer pock-eting the evidence bag. "I'll do a search."

"You got it, boss." Alma Majors. One of Battle Mountain's newest recruits. Former archaeologist turned reserve officer. There had to be a story in there, but Adan hadn't done more research than nec-essary to carry out his mission. All that mattered was Isla and Mazi, Clint's eight-year-old daughter. Getting them the hell out of this town was priority number one.

Ford disappeared into the trees as Officer Majors updated the dispatcher on their location and situa-tion. The shooter was already in the wind. If Adan was right, there wouldn't be any trace of him left be-hind, either. He was good. A professional. "You're not going to find him. You know that. You need me, Isla, and pretending you don't is only going to get you killed."

She refused to look at him.

"You know this guy?" Majors's shoulders tensed a bit more as she set him against the hood of the department's only patrol vehicle. Defensive. Came with the territory as a police officer, but his instincts said this was something more. Something deeper and learned. Past abuse, maybe?

"His name is Adan Sergeant. He's not supposed to be here." Isla straightened to her full height. She rounded out of his sight. The distinct slam of one of the truck's doors filled the night—almost as loud as that shot—before she punctured his peripheral vision with a backpack in tow. She set to work on extracting the second bullet from the truck's hood, but given what he knew of preferred ammunition, the round would've gone into the engine block.

"No sign of a shooter. I searched at least five hundred feet back." Easton Ford materialized from the shadows, not even out of breath. "No spent casings. No footprints. Guy is a ghost."

"Like I said, you aren't going to find him." Adan sat back on his cuffed wrists. "He's a professional. My guess is former marine."

"And you know this how?" Ford's gaze narrowed on him.

"My ID is in my back right pocket," he said. "I'd get it myself if I wasn't in these cuffs."

Majors searched Adan's pockets and produced his ID. She tossed it to her partner. "Meet Adan Sergeant."

The oldest Ford brother caught the wallet and pried it open. "This is a military ID. Army. Where are you currently serving?"

Long story. One he didn't want to get into now. "I'm not. Honorable discharge."

"And what are you doing in Battle Mountain?" Ford asked.

"Protecting her." Adan nodded to Isla as she turned to face him. "This is the second attempt on her life. Two shootings in as many months. He's going to try again. I'm here to make sure he doesn't succeed."

"You know Vachs." Ford motioned toward Adan with his wallet. That protectiveness was back, and Adan knew if Isla said the word, he'd find himself in a world of hurt. "How?"

Isla deposited the second bullet into a separate bag and handed it off to Easton Ford. "He's the man who got my husband killed."

Chapter Two

Her teeth pinged with a cold blast of a gasp.

"Can we hurry this up, please? I need to get out to the ranch." The pain ricocheted through her chest, but it was nothing compared to the burning sensation of taking a bullet to her side. The slab beneath her held her steady, but a funeral home was the last place she wanted to be.

The shelter-in-place order had gone into effect. All residents were to remain in their homes for the next few hours as BMPD conducted a wider search of the area. But so far, they had nothing to show for it.

"All right. Doesn't look like anything is broken, but you're going to be sore for a couple weeks." Dr. Chloe Miles stripped off a set of latex gloves and deposited them into the trash with one heeled foot on the can's pedal. Long brown hair contradicted Isla's choice to chop hers off. For a new mother, Battle Mountain's coroner managed to remain graceful and lean. She moved around her small exam room as though she'd memorized every square inch. Which she probably had, considering there wasn't much to see. "The impact could've broken your sternum. You were lucky you were wearing your vest. You can button up."

Isla did, only then aware of the scratches at the tips of her fingers. Had that happened when Adan had tackled her to the ground or when one of the bullets had shattered her window? But a better question was why did she care about tiny scrapes when the man responsible for her husband's death had suddenly manipulated his way back into her life? She'd made her position clear at the funeral. She didn't want him anywhere near her or Mazi.

"I don't have to tell you not to be alarmed by the bruising over the next few days considering what you used to do for a living, but it'll be ugly." Chloe made a note on a clipboard resting on the counter. "Better than the alternative, though. Ibuprofen for the swelling and pain. Other than that, try to get some rest."

The town's coroner wasn't usually the doctor Isla would see for something like this, but she had yet to work up her nerve to go back to the hospital. Although the back of the town's only funeral home wasn't any better. This was where she'd picked out Clint's coffin. Where they'd held the viewing.

"How's Mazi taking all this?" the coroner asked.

Isla forced herself back into the moment and fastened the top button of her uniform shirt. She cleared her throat in an attempt to block Adan from her mind.

Easton and Alma had cuffed him and taken him to the station. Soon, they'd clear him, and he'd be right back out of her life. Where he belonged. There wasn't any reason she had to keep thinking about him.

"I haven't gotten the chance to tell her." To be honest, she wasn't sure she was going to. Mazi had been so scared when Isla was shot a couple months ago. Isla didn't want to put her through that again. Thankfully, she hadn't picked up her daughter from the ranch yet the night of the first shooting, but that had been the plan just as she'd ended her shift at the firehouse. They were going to have a movie marathon to make up for all of Isla's extra shifts. But she'd never made it. Hopping down from the slab, she gathered her Taser, gun and baton and holstered them in their respective places on her belt. "Karie has been watching her up at the ranch during my shifts. As far as she knows, nothing happened. I'm sure the chief will want to fill his mom in, though. Just in case."

In case whoever had targeted Isla found Mazi.

Her heart shot into her throat all over again. In those fateful seconds after her vest had caught the bullet and the air was knocked from her lungs, all she'd thought about was her getting to her daughter. The chief had assigned both Cree and Kendric to watch over Mazi in the days after that initial shooting, and now it was happening again. Isla could only imagine the confusion and the fear her daughter must be feeling, disconnected from her.

Someone was trying to kill her.

Had shot her. Twice.

She and Mazi were in danger.

"News travels fast in a town like this. I wouldn't be surprised if my mother-in-law already knows every detail of what happened." Chloe settled her lower back against one of the counters, arms folded. "Are you regretting your decision?"

The coroner didn't have to elaborate. Isla had applied to BMPD for one reason and one reason only: to protect herself and Mazi. Tonight had answered one part of the question that had instigated her change in career. The shooting two months ago hadn't been random. But knowing that fact didn't make her feel any better. As for Adan, she had no idea how he was mixed up in this. "No. Thanks for the checkup, Doc."

"Ibuprofen and rest. I'll be by your house in a couple days to check on you," Chloe said. "Don't let me find out you're back in the field until I say so."

Wasn't going to happen. She might've gotten a partial answer to her own personal mystery. The first shooting hadn't been random, after all, but that didn't explain the gunman's motive. Or why Adan was in Battle Mountain. What were the chances of him showing up at the last second to tackle her to the ground? And had tonight been the first time? "Thanks again."

Isla wound her way toward the front of the fu-

neral home, avoiding the owner, Mr. Jacob, and his
son. Clint had been gone a year now, but the pity
in this town hadn't waned. To the people of Battle
Mountain, she was a widow and a single mother who
needed all the sympathy and help she could get. But
sympathy didn't pay the bills, and she was perfectly
capable of taking care of herself and Mazi.

Her husband's truck was still back at the rec center. The bullet she'd pulled from the engine had cut
straight through the intake manifold, according to
Cree Gregson. They'd have to tow it to the impound
lot. Not to mention the shooter had most likely removed a spark plug or her battery to stall her, putting her right where he wanted.

She should've seen it before it had been too late.
No truck meant she was on foot from here. Lucky
for her, Battle Mountain's brand-new police station
had been finished just a few weeks ago. She could
probably catch a ride out to Whispering Pines Ranch
with the chief or Easton. After that, she'd have to
figure something else out. Kind of hard to police an
entire town, even one has small as this one, without a vehicle.

In minutes, she was shoving through the glass
door and standing in the front lobby of the station.
Macie Barclay smiled up at her with straight, white
teeth, an armful of bangle bracelets jingling as she
waved at Isla. A headset decorated in bright pink
metallic nail polish rested on the dispatcher's head.

"Well, look who the cat dragged in. Heard you got into some excitement tonight."

"Could've used without." Isla leaned against the two-tier receptionist desk. "Chief in? My truck is now considered evidence, and I need a ride out to the ranch to grab Mazi."

"He's in back with someone they brought in a little bit ago. Cute, too." The brilliant, if offbeat, redhead lowered her voice. "That man's body was poetry. I wouldn't mind being his muse for a night. Or two. Might even consider breaking my celibacy streak."

A tendril of possessiveness whipped through her at the thought of Adan and Battle Mountain's dispatcher getting to know one another. "Is that a voluntary celibacy streak?"

"Is yours?" Macie narrowed her gaze.

She wasn't going to answer that with anything more than a smile. Isla headed around the front desk to the single interrogation room in the station. "I'll be back there with the chief if you need me."

"That's what I thought." Macie's laugh followed her down the hallway.

Slick white tile, white walls and white ceiling panels could've convinced a stranger she worked out of a hospital wing. The last station hadn't been so… sterilized. But considering it had been blown to hell and back by a bomber about six months ago, this was better than their temporary quarters out at Whispering Pines Ranch.

Isla set her hand over the clean silver door handle leading into the interrogation room. Adan Sergeant was on the other side of this door. Honestly, she'd expected this moment. The one where he'd find a way back into her life. That was what guilt did to a person. Made them fight boundaries everyone else had set, made them desperate to ease the pain that came with knowing what they'd done. Adan hadn't pulled the trigger that ripped Clint from her life and Mazi's, but he might as well have. Even the army knew it.

In that exact moment, the events of the night caught up with the rest of her. She hadn't stopped long enough to think about why he was in town over the fact someone wanted her dead. Isla forced herself to take a steadying breath and pushed inside.

Hazel eyes she had no business noticing locked on her. His T-shirt was too tight around the bulky muscle of his arms. Like it had been all he could find in some thrift shop. Light brown hair, cut the same exact way she remembered all those years ago, refused to step out of line. Adan was a military man through and through, and it showed. His thin lips quirked at one side as he settled back in his chair, the chief at the opposite side of the table. Right then, she knew. This wasn't an interrogation. Not to Adan. It was a joke.

"Aren't you supposed to be at the hospital getting checked out, Vachs?" Chief Ford didn't even bother looking up from the notepad in front of him as he made a note, like he'd known she would be here.

"Chloe gave me the all clear." Lie. One she wouldn't be able to sustain long, considering the chief and the coroner lived together. Isla tore her unsolicited attention from the man in cuffs. "One of the bullets went through my truck engine. I was hoping I could catch a ride out to the ranch."

A glimpse at Adan revealed exactly what she'd hoped to avoid: his undivided attention. She quickly focused on the chief as he shoved back in his chair and unpocketed a set of keys. He tossed them in her direction.

"Keep it as long as you need." Chief Ford took his seat again. "Tell Mazi I say hi."

She'd caught the keys against her chest and aggravated the impact bruises beneath her uniform. But she wouldn't show how much it hurt. Not in front of Adan. It was that pride that kept her from lunging across that table and showing him exactly what it felt like to die inside. "He give you anything?" she asked Weston.

The chief stood a second time, closing the distance between them. He maneuvered her back into the hallway and lowered his voice. "You know I can't let you investigate your own shooting, Vachs. Best you take the next few days off. Hold up with Mazi. Lie low until we have some answers. I'll call if we need you."

He was benching her.

The muscles in her jaw ached from the pressure of her back teeth. Everything she'd worked for these past few months, everything she'd tried to do for Mazi—it had been all for nothing? No. She wasn't going to just sit back and let the bastard who'd shot her try again. She wasn't going to let him put her daughter in the crosshairs. "I'll hold you to that."

A knowing expression solidified on Adan's face a split second before the chief closed the door between them. As though he understood exactly what she was thinking.

She was going to protect her family.

And no one—not even Battle Mountain PD—was going to stop her.

CHIEF FORD HAD let him go sometime around midnight.

Four hours since the shooting in the parking lot. Battle Mountain PD didn't have anything to hold him on. As far as they knew, he happened to be in the right place at the right time, but experience told him the son of a bitch who'd come after Isla was still here.

So Adan wasn't leaving. She might blame him for what happened to Clint—hell, he blamed himself—but personal feelings wouldn't be enough for him to leave her and Mazi unprotected. He owed her that much.

She'd mentioned something about catching a ride

out to the ranch while the chief had been questioning him. From what he'd been able to uncover at the town's only diner, there really was only one ranch connected to the Ford family. Whispering Pines, a bed-and-breakfast intended to give tourists a taste of the great outdoors Colorado had to offer while providing the luxury of home-cooked meals and cozy cabins. One resident had even mentioned a rehabilitation center Easton Ford had built on the property for veterans and trauma survivors to recover. It was a hell of a setup that obviously helped this town recoup from all the violence and crime that had swept through. Since Isla hadn't showed up at her house, he bet she was still there.

His feet protested as he hiked up the long drive under a giant wood sign declaring Whispering Pines Ranch overhead. A single car was parked between the semicircle of six satellite cabins and the main house with its lights still on. Considering the stickers instructing residents to call 911, he figured this was the car Isla had borrowed from the chief.

Movement registered through the main window that looked into an expansive dining room. Isla was sitting at the table, a coffee mug gripped between both hands. Her short hair shaded her face, defying her constant move to push it behind her ears. Damn, she was compelling. Even more so than he remembered. She was talking to someone in the kitchen at the back of the room. An older woman with gray-white hair, dressed in flannel and jeans. The Ford matriarch, he assumed. Isla had always been able to make friends easily. Didn't matter if she'd met them five minutes before or known them for a lifetime. She invested her entire being into keeping a relationship alive. No matter the cost. There was a light she'd always emitted that couldn't be ignored.

Until Clint had died, anyway.

"You just don't give up, do you, Sergeant?" a familiar voice asked. The too-loud crunch of gravel let Adan know Easton Ford had snuck up on him without tipping his hand. "Any reason walking up to the front door is too much for you? Or is spying one of those things that got you discharged?"

Adan instinctively raised both his hands to show he was unarmed. Good of the chief to assign someone to watch Isla, but the youngest Ford had also made it a point not to give Adan's pistol back upon release. And taken his car in for good measure. "Just out for a nice stroll, Ford. Beautiful night, don't you think?"

It wasn't. He wasn't sure at what point his toes had gone numb, but it wouldn't stop him from doing what he came here to do. He let Easton pat him down while another officer covered him from a few feet away. Cree Gregson. Seemed that after tonight, Chief Ford wasn't taking any chances.

"He's clean." Easton stood at his full height. "I didn't see another car come up the drive, which means you hightailed it all the way up here on foot from the station. That's near on six miles. What possible reason do you have for coming out here?"

Adan glanced in the window. Isla smiled through the panes, unaware of the scene outside. It would take him no less than thirty seconds—maybe a minute—to get through the two officers holding him here, but he'd learned a damn hard lesson in Morocco when Clint had died in his arms. He couldn't do this alone. He put his arms down, turning to face both officers. "You read my records."

"I still have connections." Easton nodded back toward his partner, Gregson. "We both do."

"Then you know what happened on my last assignment." Adan took a step forward, squaring his shoulders and straightening all six feet four inches of him. He came in taller than the former Green Beret, and he towered above Gregson. And he wasn't going to back down. "That woman's husband was my best friend. I convinced him to enlist with me when we turned eighteen. We served three tours together. Clint was good at what he did, but I'd watched over him my whole life. Military didn't change that. I was the sniper assigned to keep him and the rest of our unit safe."

"But something happened." Easton didn't move, didn't even seem to breathe.

That day was clear as it had happened yesterday instead of a year ago, and Adan clenched his fists to keep himself from going down that spiral of rage and loss. "Last time I saw him, something went wrong. He ended up with a chest full of lead. By the time I got to him, it was too late to do anything about it."

"You heard about the shooting." Gregson stepped into a sliver of light still emanating through the dining room. "Two months ago outside the fire station. Is that why you were here tonight? You've been watching over Clint's wife and daughter in case the shooter tried again?"

"I didn't just hear about the shooting. I was there." Adan shoved the collar of his T-shirt down, showing off the shiny, still healing tissue. "I tried to get her out of the way. The bullet went through us both. .30 caliber. I had to dig it out of my shoulder once I made sure Isla was found."

"What tipped you off she was in danger?" Easton asked.

He let go of his collar. "Two soldiers in my old unit showed up dead. Each with a .30 caliber in their chests. Then the shooter came for me three months back." He slowly extracted a chain from his front pocket. It was heavy, heavier than a civilian would think, with a sniper bullet hanging from the middle. "I pulled this from the scene and matched it to the one I dug out of my shoulder two months ago. Isla isn't part of the unit, but something told me this is tied to what happened to her husband. I was right."

Easton took it, examining how close Adan had

come to joining his best friend and the other two soldiers in his unit. ".30 caliber. You get a ballistics match?"

"I didn't need to." Doubt had lost any hold over him the past few months. "It came from the same rifle that killed those two soldiers. And Clint."

"Why Isla?" Gregson set one hand over the butt of his holstered weapon, his weight shifted to one side. "She wasn't in your unit. She doesn't have anything to do with this."

"I don't know." There were too many variables, but every single one of them connected back to that last assignment he and Clint had taken. He was sure of it. "But I'm not going to let the son of a bitch finish the job."

The front door wrenched open, and Isla stepped out fully armed and ready to take the shot. Alertness tightened the tendons along her neck and shoulders as she centered herself under the porch light. Her brilliant gaze went from Easton and Gregson to him. "Seems I'm interrupting. Someone want to tell me what the hell is going on?"

"You've got a visitor." Easton tossed the bullet back at Adan. He motioned to Gregson to retreat, and for the first time since he'd dragged her out of the shooter's line of sight, he and Isla were alone.

Isla holstered her weapon. "You followed me."

"Heard you mention something to the chief about

a ranch. Wasn't too hard to figure out which one," he said.

Right then, the fight seemed to drain out of her. It took his considerable senses to pick up the exhaustion in her voice. Something he knew she'd rather keep to herself. Not one for weakness or for letting her guard down. Especially not in front of him. "Why are you here, Adan?"

"Wanted to make sure you're okay." He motioned to her sternum. "The vest was a good idea."

Isla nearly stumbled down the porch steps.

Stress had a way of wiping out people who didn't function on it at all times. He could see it in her eyes, the paranoia, the way she scanned the trees, wondering if another bullet was headed her way. Of course, her solution had to be to become a police officer, probably assuming that would be enough to protect her. It wouldn't.

"That's not what I meant." She stood up to him, every ounce the woman he remembered. Challenge— so unlike her—flickered in her gaze, and for a split second, he wondered if he knew this woman at all. "Why are you in Battle Mountain?"

"Isn't it obvious? Someone is hunting you. They won't stop until you're dead," he said. "I'm here to make sure that doesn't happen."

"Even if I wanted you here, which I don't, I can protect myself." Isla turned to head back for the stairs. "Sorry you wasted a trip."

"Is that how you ended up in the hospital with a bullet through your side? Protecting yourself?" he asked.

She turned on him. "How do you know—" Understanding spread across her delicate features. "You. You were there that night. You're the one who tackled me to the ground." Shock replaced the puzzlement in her expression. Her oncoming steps reverberated with her anger, and she shoved her small hands into his chest. "You've been here for two months. You've been watching me, watching my daughter?"

"Yes." He didn't know what else to say.

"Who the hell do you think you are?" Her shoulders rose and fell in desperate gasps for breath. "What gives you the right to insert yourself into my life like that? I am not some girl who needs your protection, Adan. I am a cop, and we agreed you would stay away, but here you are. What were you thinking?"

They weren't getting anywhere. There was a shooter out for her blood, and he couldn't just stand here. Adan kept his voice even. "I was thinking when Clint died, I didn't just lose him on that assignment—I lost you, too. I lost Mazi, and I didn't want to go through that again. So, yeah, here I am. You might not want my help, but Clint made me swear on my life I would watch out for you. And I'm not going to fail him again. Is that good enough reason?"

Her mouth parted on a strong exhale. Five seconds. Six. She collected herself. Eyes cast to the ground, she nodded. "Yes."

"Good." He moved past her toward the cabin's front door. "Then let's get to work."

Chapter Three

They had nothing.

She slid a fresh mug onto the table. Karie Ford had gone to bed hours ago, but thankfully Isla knew how to operate the coffee machine. "Third cup's the charm."

"Thanks." Adan had set himself up with her laptop and a notepad hours ago. Two soldiers in his unit—in Clint's old unit—had been shot with the same caliber bullet as she had. The only thing that tied them all together? Her husband.

A million different scenarios had crossed her mind over the past year. What had gone wrong on that last assignment? Who'd shot Clint? Had her husband been involved in something he shouldn't have? Had his death been personal? She'd requested the details of Clint's death a thousand times. His commanding officer had never once given in. The assignment in Morocco had been deemed classified. Now she had one of the very men who'd been with Clint at the time of his death right here in front of her. She could finally get answers.

Isla took a seat at the opposite end of the table. Mazi would be awake in a few hours. She'd see Adan. She'd scream with excitement her fun uncle was back and run into his arms like she'd done so many times before. Isla could see it now, and a flicker of a smile hiked one side of her mouth higher. It didn't last. Because the questions would start then. The pain. Seeing Adan would remind Mazi that her daddy wasn't coming home. Adan would remind her of that day he'd knocked on their door dressed in his finest, his cap wedged under his arm like the good soldier he was.

They'd survived Clint's death. They'd moved on and made a new life for themselves here in Battle Mountain. They had friends, Mazi was doing amazingly well in school and Isla had a support system made up of Karie Ford, the police department and the entire fire department. All of the work they'd put into healing would be destroyed the moment Mazi set eyes on Adan.

She took a deliberate sip of her coffee and cleared her throat. "You were a sniper in the army. Is there anything at either scene you'd be able to use to tell you who we might be dealing with?"

Because the sooner they found who wanted her dead, the sooner they could get back to their lives. Her and Mazi. The two of them against the world.

"Snipers are trained to adapt to any number of variables. Wind, weather, altitude. They spend years perfecting their senses and technique." Adan leaned back in his chair, scrubbing a hand down his face. He hadn't stopped since tackling her in the parking lot—not for a second—and the wear was starting to show. On both of them. "His choice of perching in the trees was the smart move. Gave him enough cover to stay out of sight and not be recognized when he ran, but I'd have better luck ID'ing him from taking a look at his rifle."

"What would his rifle tell you?" She could do this. She could pretend they were having a normal conversation when all she wanted to think about was Adan's claim that in his final moments, Clint had made him swear to protect his wife and his daughter.

"His preferences. Which parts of the gun were customized, which eye he uses to scope. Even if he's left-handed or right-handed." Adan tipped one side of his hand away from the laptop. "Wear to certain pieces, if he changed anything out not covered by the manufacturer and how long ago they'd been done."

"So they could be traced." It made sense. Weapons—just like car engines—were etched with serial numbers. If their shooter had any custom work done on his rifle, they could use that to identify him. But they'd need the actual gun, an impossible task. The shooter wasn't going to walk into the department and hand it over because she'd asked nicely. "Did you customize your rifle?"

His gaze steadied on her, as though sensing exactly where she was going with this line of questioning. Adan wasn't police, but that didn't mean she could underestimate his ability to connect the dots. "No solider below the rank of general is allowed to customize their weapon as long as they're active duty."

"What about Morocco?" Her gut clenched. She was not entirely sure she was ready for an answer.

Adan didn't move, didn't even seem to breathe. He just looked at her, ready for the conversation they'd both avoided for the past year. "I adjusted my sights, sling and cheekpiece. Other than that, the only thing I could control was whether or not humidity rusted out and corroded my gear."

He was answering her questions to the letter, but it would take more than her dancing between the lines to get what she wanted out of him. "You told me you were responsible for Clint's death, when you showed up on my doorstep and destroyed mine and Mazi's entire world. I believed you, and I blamed you this entire time. I was content to keep on hating you, but outside you said he made you promise to watch out for us. So, what really happened on that assignment, Adan?"

His expression refused to budge. He'd been expecting this, and actually, she wasn't sure if she'd ever be able to surprise him, but he did have a tell. His left eye narrowed at the corner. Just slightly. If she hadn't been looking directly at him—if she hadn't been desperate to get some kind of reaction out of him after all this time—she would've missed it. "It was supposed to go down without a hitch. We were assigned to drop off a handful of Blackhawks and Apaches, make sure the Moroccans understood how to use them. Clint had the lead. I was watching the whole thing go down from seven hundred meters through my scope."

His voice dipped an octave, but he never broke. "I saw something to the north. It was just a flash, but enough to draw my attention from the deal. My spotter saw it, too. Another sniper in the field, one we'd missed during our first scouting. By the time I got a line of the son of a bitch, it was too late. Clint was on the ground. The Moroccans had scattered. The entire deal had gone to hell."

She forced herself to swallow through the sob building in her throat. "When you said you were responsible…"

"I couldn't protect him anymore, Isla. I'm sorry. I tried, but…" His tone changed, hinting at something more. "I left my rifle with my spotter and ran as fast as I could. Clint was still alive. Barely. He was losing blood. I tried to apply pressure, but the bullet had torn through his back. He knew he wasn't going to make it. So he made me promise. Told me I had to protect you. You and Mazi."

Tears burned in her eyes. Numbness encased the small amount of her heart she'd managed to hold on to this past year. "Protect us from what?"

"I don't know, but he obviously did." Adan shook his head. "He must've known someone would come for you."

Clint had known?

"No. He would've told me. If he knew we were in danger..." Clint wouldn't have kept her in the dark. Isla shoved away from the table. Her husband had received commendations, medals for his service. He'd served his country for years and never complained. For him, it had been an honor and a duty, and she'd been so proud of him. He was a good man. He'd never get wrapped up in something that would put his family at risk.

"Mommy?" a tiny voice called from the hallway.

Her heart sank, then shot into overdrive. "Mazi, babe, what are you doing out of bed?"

"I thought I heard Uncle Adan." Her eight-year-old, in all her wondrous curiosity and beauty, rubbed one eye with her fist while clutching a rainbow unicorn they'd found at the craft store. Blond hair tendrilled around her face in soft waves, the same color as Clint's, as she set her sights on the man at the kitchen table.

Adan stood, nodding with a brightness in his gaze

she hadn't witnessed since he and Clint had left for their last tour together. "Hey, kid."

"Uncle Adan!" Mazi pushed past Isla and made a beeline for him. "I knew you'd come back!"

Isla reached after her daughter. Too late to stop her. "Mazi, wait."

He hauled Mazi's small body against his and straightened, dragging her feet off the floor. Large hands spread across her back as he encircled her in powerful arms that had once promised to beat every boy within an inch of his life if they did Mazi wrong. "You're almost taller than me. When did you get so big, huh?"

Isla's body disobeyed every command as she stood there watching them together. Adan and Mazi's friendship had always been special. He'd been there the day she was born. He'd even brought Isla ice chips and held Mazi so she could sleep after the delivery. After a while, Mazi would only fall asleep in Adan's arms, much to the torment and pain of her parents. And much to the joy of their little family's closest friend.

A solid lump of guilt lodged in her throat that she'd kept them apart this long, but what other choice had she had? Adan had claimed responsibility for Clint's death. She couldn't look at him without thinking of what they'd lost. But now it seemed that mantle had been shouldered voluntarily. Adan had made a mistake in the field. Could she really fault him for that the rest of their lives? Could she keep Mazi away from him knowing her daughter hadn't only lost her father, she'd lost her best friend and any reminder of Clint in the same day?

Isla folded her arms across her chest, still reeling from the splintering pain of her near-death experience, and sagged against the doorframe. No matter how much she wanted to pretend Adan hadn't been part of their lives, she couldn't. Not anymore.

Someone wanted her dead, and as she watched him swing her daughter around the kitchen, Isla knew she'd need Adan now more than ever.

A FOOT PRESSED against one side of his face.

"I tried to warn you." That voice. It comprised promise and generosity, sincerity and warmth. Even at its most volatile. Isla slid onto the couch arm and took a sip from a mug. Nodding at the small human sprawled across the oversize sectional, she smiled for the first time since he'd stepped back into her life. "She's a kicker. I had to stop letting her into my bed by the time she was six."

"I can see why." Adan redirected Mazi's foot onto the pillow rather than his face. He wasn't sure when he'd finally convinced her to go to sleep last night. Not long enough ago. They'd finally fallen asleep in the living room. His head thudded with exhaustion, but he'd survived worse. He pressed himself upright.

"I thought she'd never go to sleep. What'd you give her before bed? A cup of sugar?"

"Don't look at me. You're the one who got her all riled up. Here. You look like you need this more than I do." She tossed him a banana, and he caught it against his chest. "I didn't really get a chance to thank you for last night. Although it would've been beneficiary if you'd just told me you were here to my face."

"Thanks." Adan used every ounce of his sniper training to maneuver across the sectional without alerting the sleeping girl. Muscles he'd forgotten existed tensed to keep him from waking the she-beast determined not to let him out of her sight. Once free of the sectional, he headed for the kitchen for a cup of Karie Ford's dark roast. It was the only thing that could help him recover from last night's impromptu dance party. He still didn't understand what the hell the floss was, but Mazi seemed to have it down.

"She's the train you never see coming." Isla stared through the dining room into the living room with nothing but adoration in her face. All she'd wanted to be was a mom. He'd watched her and Clint grieve through two miscarriages and fertility treatments. Then finally came Mazi, and he'd never seen his best friend or Isla so damn happy. So much in love.

"I don't know how you do this every day. She's insane." He was a trained soldier. He'd barely lasted two hours.

She turned to face him. "I fail. A lot. Whether she sees it or not. Well, actually, she likes to point out when I fail, but I like to think I do more things right than wrong."

"I'm beginning to think it takes some kind of expertise I've never heard of to succeed in the parenting department. You're way ahead of me." He gulped down his first mug of coffee and went back for a second. "How are you feeling?"

"Like Wile E. Coyote. Someone left an anvil on my chest, but I'm sure if you hadn't been there, the shooter would've gotten exactly what he wanted." She hugged her coffee mug closer, as if that was all the comfort she needed. "Mazi would've lost both parents. She would've been all alone with no one but people she barely knows to look out for her."

Adan had to suffocate the urge to reach out, to touch her. Their friendship—if he could even call it that—was still on shaky ground. Even with the truth out there. She'd spent so long hating him like he'd wanted that he wasn't sure it would ever be how it had been between them. Before Clint died. "I'm not going to let that happen, Isla."

"Yeah, well, we don't always get what we want, do we? If we did, my husband would be here." Not him. She didn't have to say the words aloud. "You never told me what made you intervene. Last night and two months ago."

"To be honest, that first night is a bit of a blur."

He leaned against the kitchen counter. "I remember waiting outside the fire station for your shift to end. It was dead quiet. I'd already searched your car. There was nothing out of the ordinary inside. Except I found broken glass on your hood."

"Broken glass?" Her attention sharpened on him.

"The streetlight above where you'd parked had been shot out." The hole in his shoulder seared in remembered agony. He rubbed at it with his free hand, but he couldn't force his body to heal any faster than he could force hers. "Before I had a chance to get to his position, you were coming out the station's front doors. I ran to intervene, but the shooter... He'd already taken the shot."

Isla set her mug on the dining room table and closed the distance between them. Before his brain had a chance to connect the dots, she tore at his collar and exposed the shiny scar tissue underneath. Her face lost any hint of color. "The bullet went through you first."

His skin grew hot where she'd touched him. "You were there on the ground. I tried to keep you awake, but you were bleeding out, and I was right back there with Clint, watching him die."

She retreated, that brilliant gaze of hers scanning the entire room instead of sticking with him. Isla swiped at the line of tears in her eyes. "Why didn't you just tell me?"

He pressed his shirt collar back into place. "You

told me to go away and never come back. I tend to follow orders."

"Yet here you are," she said. "What about last night?"

"The last thing I saw before Clint was shot was a glint of metal. Not part of a rifle. No professionally trained shooter would add something like that to his weapon, and the military sure as hell wouldn't allow it. It had to be something else. Like a necklace or a medal the shooter wears. Some snipers use good-luck charms. I think this guy might be one of them." He still hadn't been able to make out the shape, but one of the townspeople's headlights had skimmed those trees at the end of the meeting last night and there it had been. Bright as day.

Isla stepped forward. The possibility of a lead practically buzzing. "You saw it. Last night. You saw the same thing you did that day in Morocco."

"Yes, and I was almost too late again." Adan couldn't fight it anymore. He countered her retreat, gripping both hands on her arms to prove she was really here and not just a figment of his imagination. "If you hadn't been wearing your vest—"

"Why now?" she asked. "Why two months ago? Clint has been dead a year. If the shooter is somehow tied to him, he's had plenty of opportunities and time to come after me. What makes these past couple months so special?"

"I don't know, but we have to assume he'll try

again." He already had a plan in place. "Both you and Mazi have to leave Battle Mountain. Now. I've got a place we can lie low outside of town for a few weeks before we head out of state. Should give us enough time to hide our trail."

Defiance flashed in her eyes, and she wrenched out of his hold. "No."

His hands burned where his skin had made contact with hers. "Isla, this isn't a game—"

"You don't get it, do you? The life we have here? It's ours. Mine and Mazi's. We had to build it from the ground up after Clint died. We had to figure it out on our own, and we've worked too hard to have it taken from us now. She's finally not having nightmares. She loves school. She has friends and is learning how to ride horses out here on the ranch. I can't take that from her, Adan." She shook her head. "We're not leaving. Whatever plan you have to find this shooter, I'm all for it, but we're not running. I don't care who's trying to kill me. No one gets to upend my family's life again."

She headed for the living room. "Time to get up and have some breakfast, baby girl."

Mazi's sleep-laden voice reached him in the kitchen. "Is Uncle Adan still here?"

Adan almost stepped out from the kitchen, but this was a conversation between mother and daughter. A relationship he had no part in anymore.

Isla's voice softened. "Yeah. He is, but just for a

little while. Come on. I'll fix you something while you get dressed."

"Is he staying with us while he visits?" the eight-year-old tornado asked.

Adan's entire body went still as he waited for an answer. As much as his promise to Clint ruled his post-military life, he wasn't sure staying in his best friend's home, with the man's wife and daughter, was the best option.

"You know what, I thought we could stay here at the ranch for a couple days," Isla said.

It wasn't a bad idea, either. He hadn't gotten the chance to survey the entire property last night, but from what he'd read about this place, it was well se-cured. Especially between Chief Ford and the former Green Beret still positioned out front. "You can fol-low Karie around and help with chores and making meals for all those hungry officers and tourists that come through here. Won't that be fun?"

"Yeah!" The excitement bled from Mazi's voice after a moment. "But where will Uncle Adan go?"

"Uh, I'm…not sure." Seconds slipped in silence.

Adan stepped into sight.

"I'll just be right outside in one of the other cab-ins, kiddo." He cut his attention to Isla to gauge her reaction, but she'd already thrown up those defensive walls again. Adan tossed the banana she'd given him between both hands like a football. "You can come visit me whenever you want, if that's okay with your mom."

Mazi looked to her mother for confirmation. In that moment, he saw the hesitation in her eyes. What was she supposed to do? Say no? Isla nodded. "Sure. It'll be…fun. Now go get ready like I said."

Mazi bounced off the sectional as though she hadn't lost almost an entire night of sleep and gut-checked him with a headfirst hug. It had been a long time since someone a third of his size could bring him down, but the eight-year-old was an expert. "It'll be just like when you used to come visit. We're going to have a sleepover!"

"I can't wait." Adan patted her back and sent her off.

Isla's phone rang. She answered the call, but he saw in the flash of her eyes the warning and exasperated look she'd always given him for indulging Mazi. "Vachs."

Adan busied himself with shoveling the banana down his throat as she spoke in low tones, but something in the way her shoulders drew together down her back set him on edge. He'd always been able to read her. Time hadn't made an exception.

She ended the call.

"Everything okay?" Instinct had him stepping toward her, ready for the fight.

"That was Macie, our dispatcher. She's been trying to reach me on the radio." Isla dropped her phone into her slacks and grabbed her coat off the back of one of the dining room chairs. Threading both arms into the sleeves, she armed herself. "The call came in last night. A body in town. Shot with a .30 caliber bullet."

Chapter Four

"Victim is Gail Oines. Sixty-three. She's listed as the owner of the property." Kendric Hudson, looking fresh off toddler duty, led her through the massive collection of garbage, trinkets and magazines stacked nearly ceiling-high in every direction. His usually styled hair fell out of place, and he'd let his beard grow a bit longer than she was used to. Guess that was what happened when you suddenly became a parent. Sleepless nights, lowered expectations, thousands of baby wipes.

She didn't miss those days, but at the same time, Mazi had grown up way too fast. Her eight-year-old had taken on adult feelings of grief and rage and loss and become something Isla had never expected. A young woman. Soon they'd have to talk about a whole lot of changes on top of what they'd already been through. What Isla wouldn't give to go back and rewrite history, give her daughter the years of childhood she deserved.

A musty smell permeated her pores as she tried to

follow the path Kendric had set up to direct her and other officers to the body. Taking care to not topple the paper skyscrapers threatening to collapse at any moment, they reached the back bedroom through an equally suffocating hallway. Adan, too large for the packed space, followed on her heels. He was close. Too close, but the slight, clean scent of whatever soap he'd used recently settled her gag reflex.

Kendric motioned to a thick steel door where the hallway had suddenly gotten colder. "From what we can tell, the perp picked the lock on the garage door and entered through the house here. There's evidence of a struggle, as you can see. Oines fought back before he dragged her into the bedroom."

It took her a minute to understand what Kendric was pointing out amid the collection. Stacks of old mail lined one wall, but two piles had been knocked to the stained blue carpet. Frames tilted on their edges behind the stacks, and Isla caught sight of a family photo. Hard to imagine an entire family living here, but considering the condition of the home, she bet their victim hadn't seen anyone in a long time. Gail Oines. The name didn't sound familiar at all, but that wasn't altogether surprising as Isla and Mazi had only moved back from military life to Battle Mountain a year ago. Still. How was a sixty-three-year-old woman connected to the shooter stalking this town? "How long ago?"

"Call came in around one this morning. Chloe is

examining the body now. She should have something for us." Kendric pushed into the bedroom ahead of them.

1:00 a.m. Around the time Isla had stopped fighting to keep Adan from sliding back into her life. Now Mazi wouldn't let him leave. Awareness bristled along the back of her neck as Adan walked behind her. It wasn't just the hint of soap she noticed. He'd always had a presence she couldn't ignore. When Adan Sergeant entered a room, you noticed. Everyone noticed. Only this time, she felt it even more. Like a physical stroke up her spine.

Isla rounded into the bedroom, immediately assaulted by the coppery sweet scent of blood and the beginning stages of decomposition. Gail Oines lay back in the recliner beside her bed as though she'd just sat down to watch the small black-and-white television with bunny ears on the dresser. The glasses Isla had noted in the family photo lay crippled on the floor at her feet. Small but full lips parted under a frozen expression of pain and horror as the victim stared up at the popcorn ceiling. The wound in her chest was smaller than Isla expected, but based on the amount of blood soaked into the chair and from personal experience, she bet the bullet had done a lot more damage on exit. Her side burned in remembered agony and fear, and she took a physical step back to detach mentally. And bumped straight into Adan. Isla countered on instinct, clearing her throat.

"Dr. Miles, this is Adan Sergeant. Adan, Dr. Miles. He has experience with shooters like the one we're looking for."

"I'd shake your hand, but I'd rather not contaminate any evidence." Chloe retracted some kind of device with a long thin needle. The machine beeped, and the coroner made a note on the pad of paper off to her right. "I'm putting time of death between eleven p.m. and one a.m. last night. One shot through the chest. Entry wound matches the damage of a .30 caliber round, but I won't know for sure until the autopsy or we find the bullet. From what I've seen of this place, though, it might take a while. She's got defensive wounds on her hands and patches of hair missing from her scalp. Fresh. Whoever did this was pulling chunks."

"Call came in at twelve p.m. to report the body. Narrows it down," Kendric said. "Torture?"

"It wasn't a quiet kill, I can tell you that." Dr. Miles got to her feet. "As of right now, all I can say is this was homicide. Barring any surprises, I'd bet the bullet through her chest led to exsanguination. Once we get her back to the exam room, I'll fingerprint her and have Dr. Corsey pull any dental X-rays she might've had done in the past. Get you a positive ID."

Adan just stood there. Silent as a ghost. Observing. But not the body. No. Instead he was studying the perfectly stacked books lining the walls of this room. For a hoarder, Gail Oines obviously had a system.

"You think the killer made the call?" Isla asked.

"He wouldn't want to draw attention to himself or what he's been doing. From what I've been able to tell, he's on a one-man mission. Prefers to work alone. Was maybe even disciplined for not being able to get along with others." Adan circled around the end of the bed with its oversize wood frame and took position in front of the overflowing closet, his back to them all. "Your victim was tortured for information. You can't see the bruises yet, but give it a few hours. The shooter wanted something from her, then he cleaned up anything that could lead back to him."

"If he didn't make the call, then someone else might have been here at the time of the shooting." Isla scanned the room. If that was the case, they weren't just looking for a shooter. The manhunt would start for a witness. She stopped near the obsessively clean nightstand on the other side of the bed near where Adan stood. That was odd. Out of everything in this entire house, why keep one nightstand clean? She followed in Adan's footsteps. "This nightstand is probably the cleanest piece of furniture I've seen in the entire house. No dust." She bent down and inhaled. "Recently polished. I'd say Mrs. Oines uses this one, but the books in progress are on the other table"

The weight of Adan's attention burned between her shoulder blades.

The clothes in the closet. They hadn't been tossed inside. They'd each been folded neatly and stacked. Several pairs of jeans, shirts. Shoes lined up against one another. Preserved. That was the word that came to mind, and a familiar ping registered in her chest. "Her husband died. She still keeps his clothes, all these books. Even makes sure his nightstand is how he left it."

She couldn't fault Gail Oines for that. Isla hadn't been able to get rid of anything of Clint's. Not his truck. Not his military uniforms. There were boxes of files and training material she couldn't even bear to shred. Instead, she'd dragged them halfway across the country when she and Mazi had come to Battle Mountain. Was this what she would become if left unchecked? Would she be so desperate to hold on to anything she could of Clint's and the life they'd created together? Would Mazi want anything to do with her then? Uncertainty lodged in her throat, and Isla straightened to face the three sets of eyes locked on her. "We can rule out the call being made by a spouse."

"Snipers wear earplugs to prevent damage to their ears from multiple shots. Shooting a gun is louder than civilians expect" Adan seemed to have gotten closer to her over the past few minutes. "Neighbors would've heard it. Most likely one of them called it in."

"I've already questioned the families on either side." Kendric unpocketed a small notebook and pen from his breast pocket. "These guys to the north are out of town until the end of the week, and the ones to the south said they were woken up by something, but that they thought it was a car backfiring. They're not the ones who called it in, and Macie couldn't get the guy to give his name during the call. We're still making our way through the canvas. Maybe something will pop."

Adan stood a bit taller, and Isla's gut told her something Kendric said had gotten his attention. "Shooter would've known that."

"Known what?" she asked.

"About the neighbors on vacation. He would've done his own surveillance before coming in here. Would've watched the victim, memorized her habits and routines," he said. "What better place to keep an eye on your target than from right next door?"

"I'll get us access right now." Kendric brought his phone to his ear and stepped out into the hallway.

Isla couldn't take her eyes off the nightstand or the gold wedding band she'd just noticed hanging from the top of the lamp on a chain. She wouldn't touch it. Anything and everything in this room could be considered evidence, and she wasn't going to contaminate any chance of stopping this bastard from hurting someone else.

"You okay?" Adan's voice rumbled through her as though he were pressed against her. It held the perfect hint of concern while reminding her they were in the middle of a crime scene.

"I'm fine." She focused on the case at hand. Not the one that had haunted her life over the past year. Isla pointed out the bedroom door. "Gail Oines has family pictures. I think there's a son in one of them. Might take a bit of doing to identify him, though. Who knows if she kept personal records or anything like that here."

Adan released her from his gravitational pull as he headed back for the hallway. He made sure not to trample any of the mail that had fallen free from the struggle between the victim and the shooter, and a surge of appreciation flooded through her. He wasn't an investigator. He'd been a sniper in the military, but that meticulous training bled into consideration for her job and the woman in the recliner. He wiped dust off one of the photos pinned behind a stack of mail almost as tall as him. Then leaned closer.

It wasn't much, but she caught the slight change in his expression and stepped closer to get a better look. "What is it?"

"We can stop searching the house." Adan removed the photo from the wall and turned it to face her. "I know exactly why the shooter was here."

LAYTON BURGESS.

Records showed Gail Oines had once been married to the soldier's father, Jerry Burgess, but upon divorce and remarrying, she'd since taken her deceased husband's name. Oines.

That was why he hadn't made the connection right away, but the pieces were coming together.

Sergeant Layton Burgess had been assigned security on his last tour to Morocco. Right along with Clint and Adan. Only instead of going after Burgess directly, the shooter had set up shop next door to the man's mother. Why? As leverage? Hoping for a lead on her son? Or had his target managed to evade capture and Burgess's mother had paid the price?

Adan watched his step as he took in the spotless scene. So different from the house next door. But he was willing to bet Gail Oines's next-door neighbors, the Carmichaels, weren't usually this fastidious about their home. The shooter would've cleaned up after himself after he'd finished the job. Taken the trash with him, wiped down any fingerprints he'd left behind. Scrubbed away any evidence he'd been here. Without a crime scene unit on staff, processing the scene would fall to BMPD. They wouldn't get anything from this place.

"The sheets and pillowcases are missing from the bed." Isla's soft footprints kept him in the present as she returned to the main living space, kept at bay the building guilt and anger he'd tried to control. It wasn't enough that Clint had been targeted. Now his entire unit was in the crosshairs. Men and women he'd die to protect, if given the chance. Worse, Isla was in this bastard's sights. She was beginning to resemble Gail Oines more than he wanted to admit. A widow hunted by a shooter who had information he'd kill to get his hands on. But the latest victim didn't have an eight-year-old relying on her. She hadn't had an entire life ahead of her.

Adan wouldn't let Isla end up like her.

"He took them with him." They wouldn't find anything here. Whoever had been on the other side of the rifle that killed Gail Oines was long gone and knew what he was doing. But considering BMPD hadn't gotten a second call about a body, hope that Layton Burgess was still alive thrived. "Same with the trash and his shell casings at the scene. I'll bet he found the bullet, too. He didn't want anything connecting him back to the scene next door." Adan crouched, skimming his hands over the carpet in the front room. "Even wore booties to distort his boot tread."

They weren't just dealing with a run-of-the-mill sniper spat out of the military. This was a professional contractor. Someone who'd been in the field during Adan and Clint's last assignment together. Who was there the day his best friend was shot and killed.

"Kendric is searching Layton Burgess's apartment as we speak. No sign of him yet." Isla feathered her hands over a white farmhouse-style TV stand. Her phone rang from her pocket, and she reached to dig it free. "Vachs."

Adan swept through the rest of the living room.

"Yes, sir. I understand." Her voice dipped, drawing Adan's attention. "I'll be there as soon as I can." She ended the call with a curse under her breath and turned back to the scene. "What are the chances another soldier from Clint's unit ends up in Battle Mountain? This place…it's the middle of nowhere. Barely on the map."

Something had changed. "Who was on the phone?"

"It's not important." Isla shook her head and pocketed her phone, as if saying, *out of sight, out of mind.* "We were talking about why Layton Burgess was here."

"Could be the isolation is exactly why he chose to come here. Maybe it had something to do with Clint being from here or because his mother was here. I don't know yet." Or… Maybe Layton Burgess's connection to Battle Mountain had something to do with Isla. The soldier had been born and raised back east. Adan remembered the operator telling stories about his parents forcing him to visit every national park they could drive to within a day. Dozens of road trips down the coast and through the South. Burgess hadn't appreciated it at the time, but he could see how his parents had helped prepared him for joining the military. But what had happened to make him come to Colorado? What brought Gail

Oines? "Did he ever come around? Call? Reach out to you or Mazi?"

"Burgess?" She kept searching for signs of the shooter. She wouldn't find them, but for the first time since he'd tackled her in that parking lot, Isla didn't seem to be making it a point to get as far from him as possible. "Not that I know of. I didn't even know someone else who knew Clint was here."

"This place is too clean." He took position in the small dining room with one window that faced Gail Oines's home. From here, he had a perfect view into the victim's living room on one end of the house and the bedroom at the other end, where she'd been found. It also gave him a view of a set of ATV tracks at the side of the house, but there wasn't an ATV in sight. "Our best chance of getting ahead of the shooter is to find Layton Burgess."

"How do we do that?" She ducked right beside him to take a look at Oines's home, and the part of him that had always been envious of Clint growled to life.

She and Clint had been perfect together, the all-star couple out of their group of friends. They'd hosted dinners, brought the best desserts to the barbecues, arranged the get-togethers after the tours ended, and made sure to keep in touch with everyone. They'd sent Christmas cards and set up a guest room in case anyone wanted to visit. There'd been pictures of them and Mazi in the yard, at the swimming pool, on vacation. In every single one of them, she and Clint had been smiling. So obviously in love.

It wasn't Isla he'd wanted for himself. It was the life she and Clint had built together. He'd never had that kind of connection with another person. Someone who looked at him the way she'd looked at his best friend. The fact they'd made one hell of a kid in the process was just an extra kick to the gut. And he couldn't leave that little girl without a father and a mother. "*We* aren't. You're still considered a target as long as this guy is out there, and I seem to recall your chief telling you that you can't investigate your own shooting. You should go back to the ranch. Check in on Mazi. I'll call you if I find anything."

In truth, he knew men like Layton Burgess as well as he knew himself. If Burgess had gone to ground as Adan suspected, especially if he'd learned his mother had been murdered in search of him, he'd be on the defense and ready to wage war against anyone who came looking for him. He wasn't going to let Isla get caught in the crossfire. No. Adan had to approach Burgess alone. Convince him he wasn't the man gunning for him and figure out what the hell was going on.

She moved to argue.

"Please, Isla." A surge of emotion he didn't want getting between them flashed hot and wild. "I already lost my best friend and two other soldiers in my unit. I can't lose you and Mazi, too."

"That's the problem, Adan. We're not yours to lose, remember? You might be out of the military, but you're just following another set of orders. Same as me." She raised her chin in defiance, pegging him with dark eyes as she tugged her keys free from her slacks. She didn't wait for him to respond. Because he couldn't. "I'm coming with you. I just need to make a quick stop first."

She headed for the door.

Hell. No matter how many times Clint had talked about his wife's stubbornness, Adan had never believed him. He was starting to think his best friend had underestimated Isla's determination. And he couldn't even fault her for it. She wanted answers, just as he did. What gave him the right to try to stop her from getting them?

Adan followed her out the door after making sure the Carmichael home was secure. The shooter wouldn't come back here—too risky—but Adan wouldn't take the chance of squatters or burglars breaking in while the family was still on vacation.

He settled in the passenger-side seat of Weston Ford's patrol cruiser. The cabin had filled with her light scent as she'd waited for him, stronger now that the heater was blowing full blast. Something citrusy and compelling. Just like her.

"Where to?" His knees butted against the glove compartment, even with his seat positioned all the way back.

Isla scrolled through the call history on the mobile digital terminal positioned between them. "I need to stop by the courthouse. The mayor wants to question me about the shooting from last night."

"The mayor? Isn't that a little above his pay grade?" he asked.

"You'd think so, but he made his intentions to investigate the department at the town hall meeting last night very clear." Isla slowed her taps on the keyboard. "Guess he's following through."

Adan caught another look at the ATV tracks along the side of the Oines's house. There was a strong possibility Burgess had discovered his mother's murder, called police, then fled from the shooter on the four-wheeler. Out here in wild country, an ATV wouldn't have been the smart choice. But that left the matter of Burgess's initial vehicle, the one he'd arrived in. Would the shooter have taken it? Adan would have, in his position. Every detail he learned about his target—including what he drove, what kind of snacks he consumed, choice in air freshener—could lead him in the right direction. He commandeered the terminal. "We need to find out what kind of car Burgess drives and issue an all-points bulletin."

"You remember I'm a cop, right? This is kind of what I do for a living now." She maneuvered the monitor back in her direction. Long fingers tapped across the keyboard with a speed he'd never had the acuity to reach. Seemed every time he looked in her direction, she revealed a new layer, a new talent, a new side of her he hadn't noticed before. "I already took care of it while you were taking your sweet time inside. We're looking for a red four-door sedan. Late model. No reports of abandoned vehicles, but I've got the entire department on the lookout."

He was impressed. All this time he'd wondered if she'd rushed into this career change out of fear. She was an EMT, for crying out loud. She'd spent years learning how to save people's lives, and she'd done a damn fine job of it. Clint hadn't shut up about how proud he was of her. No matter where they'd been stationed, Isla had managed to engrain herself and their family into the rescue community. Because that was what they'd been. Rescuers. At least for him. Now it seemed there was a part of her, at least, that had taken her police training to heart, and Adan's own brand of pride bubbled to the surface.

The realization should've come with a sense of relief, but all he could think about was the possibility of finding her and Mazi with a set of matching .30 caliber bullets despite that training. The shooter they were up against didn't stay within the bounds of the law. Wouldn't think twice about shooting a cop. Or a child. As long as it served the bastard's purposes, every target was fair game. Isla was a target, time was running out and he wasn't going to leave her to go this alone. "In that case, take me to your leader."

Chapter Five

Well, that had been a complete waste of time.

Isla wrenched open the glass door to her favorite bakery. She needed chocolate. Fast.

Her interview with the mayor had turned into an interrogation the moment she'd stepped into his office. *What was Chief Ford like in the field? Have you ever noticed him break protocol? What about any other of your fellow officers?* She'd kept her cool in order to keep this job, but frustration wasn't so easily neutralized. No questions about the shooting, how she was holding up or if they'd uncovered any leads. It had all been about the department as a whole. Looking for a broken scale to take advantage of before gutting the beast.

The bittersweet scent of chocolate filled her lungs. That helped.

Caffeine and Carbs was smaller than it used to be.

The excruciating rebuild had taken too long, according to the owner and baker, Reagan. And the insurance money had run out too soon. It was still a whole new world once she and Adan stepped through the door. The bell overhead chimed with their entrance, and like one of Pavlov's dogs, her mouth watered for the sweet pastries residents couldn't get anywhere else in town.

Canelés, glassy opera cakes, an entire rainbow of macarons with sweet frosted filling. Isla headed past the maze of small round tables and chairs and straight for the pastry case. A single outline popped up from behind the brightly lit platform meant to tempt everyone who walked by the window overlooking Main Street. "You know why I'm here."

"Officer Vachs, good morning." Reagan Allen hefted a small white box over the case with one hand and closed the sliding case door with the other. Battle Mountain's only baker didn't look like a once world-class creative who'd competed with the top pastry chefs in Paris, but he sure baked like one. As far as she knew. Not like she'd ever been to France or anywhere outside the United States, but she nearly cried every time she bit into one of his sweet treats, and that was good enough for her. "Already packaged and ready to go. You didn't think I'd forget about you, did you?"

"Sweet, sweet decadence." She almost shook at the possibility of taking this back to the car and shoving her face into the box like some wild raccoon. Isla handed off cash. She didn't actually want to know how much she spent on *viennoiseries* filled with flaky layers and chocolate when she looked at her credit card statement. "Thanks, Reagan. You're a magician."

"I take it you've been here before." Adan's hazel gaze brightened with the help of the overhead lights. That ridiculous and charming closed-lip smile of his said he wanted to laugh but thought better of it under the circumstances.

"A few times." If he thought she would share even a single bite of her breakfast, he was mistaken. The only person who'd ever gotten the pleasure was Mazi, and it took everything Isla had to give in to her daughter's pleas. "I recommend the eclairs. You won't find them anywhere else in Battle Mountain."

Adan took her recommendation as she maneuvered through the too-small tables peppering the too-small bakery. Hints of cinnamon, butter and sugar filled her lungs. She took a seat near the floor-to-ceiling bookcase stocked with all kinds of reads. Romance, thrillers, those mysteries she'd listened to as a kid about two Siamese cats helping their owner solve cases. Once upon a time, this place had seemed as foreign as another country. This small piece of heaven off Main Street had helped her adjust.

Isla pried open the pastry box just as Adan took a seat across from her. His knees struck hers, and it took everything she had not to laugh at the ridiculousness of him sitting at one of these tables a third of his size. Then came the realization he hadn't moved his knee from hers. She forced herself to focus on the facts. As much as it pained her to admit, Adan was here to keep her from getting shot for a third—and most likely final—time. This wasn't a coffee date. They weren't here as friends or to catch up. Gail Oines had died presumably trying to protect her son, and the madman responsible was still out there.

Could be putting Isla in his sights through the bakery's front window right now.

She stared down at her *viennoiserie*, and a low ringing started in her ears. Her side pinged with remembered pain, even though the wound hadn't bothered her in over a week. The bruises over her sternum, though… They'd last a while. So was he out there now? The shooter. Was he watching her every move through the window? Just waiting for the right time to finish his mission?

"Clint used to buy those for you when he came home from tour." Adan took a bite of his eclair and somehow managed to prevent all the filing from coming out the other end. Pure magic in her opinion. Then again, everything he did seemed to have a kind of grace. Something a man his size and background shouldn't have. Like a shark fin cutting through the water without disturbing the surface. "They're your favorite."

His voice ripped her back into the present, and the thought he'd purposefully interrupted her destructive downward spiral crossed her mind. Which was impossible. Wasn't it? She took another bite of her pastry, trying not to melt into a puddle on the new floor for Reagan to clean up later. "My grandmother used to make them for me whenever my brother and I visited her house. Sometimes with raisins, but I prefer chocolate. This place has the best, though. The first time Clint brought me one was after his first tour. He'd dropped me and Mazi here with his parents and left for Afghanistan. When he got home, I think he was afraid I'd leave him for Reagan. I mean, I thought about it. Why buy them from the baker when you can have the baker right at home?"

"What? Reagan isn't your type?" Adan made a mock attempt to turn in his chair to check out the baker serving up samples to a sweet family that had come in behind them. "Come on, look at those big brown eyes."

"You're forgetting about the four-foot ponytail." She chewed around her mouthful of decadence and butter. "I don't want to think about what that guy's shower drain looks like."

Adan's laugh lit up the entire room, claiming the attention of the family at the pastry case, and she couldn't help but smile at the lightness he imbued. It was a rare and beautiful thing. In that moment, the guilt, the fear, the hardness—it was gone. Leaving behind pure Adan. The one she'd known before their worlds had crumbled. "Is that why you came back to Battle Mountain? The bakery?"

Her smile slipped, and Isla set down the remnants of the *viennoiserie*. She wiped the chocolate from her fingers to give her a few seconds to recover. "No. It's not."

"You came back for Clint." The heaviness was back in his expression.

"Stupid, right? Dragging Mazi here, thinking this is where we could remember him the best. Like he's part of this town or something." At the time of his death, it had been all she could think about. Getting her husband back. Figuring out some way to be close to him again. In vain. Clint came from Battle Mountain, but that wasn't where he'd lived his life. It was with her and Mazi. In North Carolina, in Washington, DC, West Virginia, Alabama, Texas. The moves were hard, leaving was hard every time, but the three of them had always had each other. This place just… It felt like him.

Adan reached across the table. His hand engulfed both of hers. Warmth bled from his palm and worked to ease her grip around her napkin. He stared at her dead-on, not letting her back away or run. "It's not stupid to try to hang on to those we've lost, Isla. It's how we survive the pain."

Right then, she wasn't sure if they were still talking about Clint or the cracks that had widened in their own friendship. Her hands grew hot under his. Her brain told her she needed to pull away, but there was a part of her that needed that warmth. Needed to be the center of someone's attention. Needed to be wanted by someone else other than her eight-year-old. And Adan… He felt good. Solid. Like he could keep the entire world together if he set his mind to it.

She pulled her hands into her lap as a surge of her own guilt threatened to pull her to pieces. Clint hadn't been gone a year, and here she was having coffee and pastries with his best friend. Isla shoved to her feet, napkins and untouched coffee in hand. "I'm going to check the blotter. See if someone has spotted Layton Burgess's vehicle."

Distance. She needed distance. She tossed her garbage into the container by the door and ignored Reagan's farewell as she shoved outside. Cool mountain air drove into her lungs. She didn't make it to the patrol car. Her legs refused to move. No matter how many times men had flirted with her or asked her out—especially the firefighters at the station—while Clint had been on tour, she'd never fed into it. She'd been faithful through and through. She'd loved him, and she wouldn't have ever risked losing what they had.

Clint might not be here anymore, but the thought of moving on, of forgetting him to live out her life with someone else… No. She couldn't do that to him.

The bell chimed over the door behind her.

She didn't have to turn to know Adan had followed her out. Did she have to explain? Exhaustion and a whole lot of emotion surrounding this case and her grief had gotten the best of her. She didn't want to get into talking about her feelings. To anyone.

Adan stopped beside her. Almost two feet away. "I'm sorry."

"What?" Isla raised her gaze to his.

"For touching you. I'm sorry." He studied the slow movements of Main Street. Looking for danger? Avoiding eye contact? His expression was too unreadable to know. "I was following my instincts, thinking it would make you feel better, but it obviously didn't sit well with you. It won't happen again."

Surprise lanced through her, and she did her own scan of the center of town. Not to narrow down potential threats. To cover the abrupt sense of rejection she felt at the thought of being cut off from that warmth all over again. But cutting herself off was for the best. Because no matter how much she craved to be loved like Clint had loved her, Adan wouldn't ever fit the bill. She headed for her patrol car. "Thank you."

Isla collapsed into the front seat, taking command of the terminal as Adan got in. The entire car shifted to the passenger side from his weight alone. There was a metaphor in there somewhere. How everyone seemed to lean into him whether they wanted to or not. But not her. She brought up the all-points bulletin and started the car. Finally. A lead. "Good news. Someone just spotted Layton Burgess's vehicle."

"This isn't creepy at all." Isla slammed the driver's-side door behind her, one hand on the butt of her weapon. "Looks like nobody has lived here in years."

Adan's fingers tingled to have a weapon of his own as he shouldered out of the patrol car, but he wasn't military anymore. And Chief Ford had taken away his gun until he'd finished interrogating Ada's superiors as to his mental state and movements since his discharge.

The small yellow box that had once been considered a house almost bled into the background of the landscape. Heat from the desert sun rippled across the ground and distorted the flat roof and covered porch. But looks could be deceiving. That was one of the first lessons he'd learned the hard way. Especially when a security operator from the military was involved. Layton Burgess's red four-door sedan sat exactly where the anonymous tipster had claimed, but something didn't feel right here. Too isolated. Too open. "Any luck requesting backup?"

"The chief has the baby today since Dr. Miles is doing the autopsy for Gail Oines. Easton had to drive Genevieve back to Alamosa for her next case. Cree and Alma responded to a possible break-in at Hopper's Hardware, and Kendric is still processing Layton Burgess's house."

He didn't like this. "Any lead on who owns this place?"

"The property records are jumbled. Bunch of shell corporations that will take weeks to unravel." She kicked at a construction bucket that had escaped with a gust of wind. "Can't imagine anyone would want to hang on to a place like this. There's nothing out here but miles of dirt, scrub brush and mountains."

A once-white porch swing protested as the wind changed direction. Layton Burgess's tire treads had been wiped away. No way to tell which direction he'd come from, where he'd gone or if he'd left at all. The shooter had tortured Burgess's mother for information, which meant they needed to find Burgess. The former security operator was somehow connected to this case. They'd have to search the house. Without backup.

Adan took in the glint of new hardware on the front door. Chances were, they approached that door, they'd get shot. "Take cover behind the car and don't move until I tell you otherwise."

"You seem to keep forgetting I'm the police officer here." Isla unholstered her weapon. "I'm the one with the gun."

Now wasn't the time to argue. "And I'm the one who's worked with this guy. He's paranoid on another level. Add to that his mother just showed up dead, tortured, and he's bound to shoot anyone he doesn't recognize."

The fight drained from her shoulders. "Fine, but I'm keeping the gun."

"I won't need it." Adan faced off with the front door, still about thirty feet away. He took a single step. Then another. The weight of being watched settled in his chest. Clouds of dust kicked up behind him and swept through an entire grove of Joshua trees. "Burgess!"

His voice faltered on another violent gust of wind.

"It's me. Sergeant." Adan raised his hands in surrender, taking another step. "I'm not here to hurt you. I'm not the one who shot your mother."

No answer.

He approached the front door from a different angle, catching sight of what looked like a shed behind the main structure of the house. Nothing but desert to the horizon. They were ten miles from town. Far enough away nobody would notice a former soldier missing. If Layton Burgess hadn't driven that car out here, the shooter had, and they were walking straight into a trap. It was the smart move. Get all the targets in one place and take them out one by one.

Adan stopped dead cold. And he'd brought Isla into the open. Hell. What had he been thinking? He should've zip-tied her, carried her off the ranch and put her in the safe house when he'd had the chance. She would've fought him the entire way, but she'd have been safe.

He glanced back toward her taking cover at the back of the patrol car, her dark gaze alert and wide. She nodded. She had his back. Despite the anger and the pain and the grief, he trusted her to pull the trigger when it counted. Adan stepped onto the creaking front porch. A single picture window coated in years of dust reflected his movements, but with the curtains drawn, he couldn't get a good look inside. No telling what waited for him on the other side of the door, but someone had been here. Recently. No other reason to put in a new dead bolt.

With another glance back at Isla, he compressed the ornate door handle with his thumb. The door swung open. No security operator would leave his safe house unsecured, if that was what this place was. Then again, maybe the shooter had manipulated them from the beginning. Luring them into a false sense of security with these leads. "Only one way to find out."

For Isla and Mazi's sake.

Isla kept low as she left cover, sending his nerves into overdrive. Faster than he thought possible, she'd taken position behind him, and a small sense of ease washed through him.

He crossed the threshold first. Dust dislodged from the doorway and rained down in a thin veil of gold glitter as sun penetrated through the back windows. Dark trim, dark wood, dark floors. Not much of an entryway. A bare living room with nothing more than a worn upholstered chair off to the left. Ahead, a scarred family-sized table took up most of the open kitchen.

"Look." Isla kept her voice low, nodding at the floor. "Footprints. Size nine, maybe ten. Burgess's?"

Adan tested the light switch just inside the door. Didn't work. "I don't know, but I doubt he's the one who called in the anonymous tip telling us where to find his car."

"What is this place?" She lowered her weapon. Moving into the kitchen, she tipped a box of cereal over on the counter. Then froze.

No sign of an ambush. Nothing to suggest they weren't alone. Still, he didn't trust the situation. Why lure him and Isla all the way out here with a false tip other than to get her in the shooter's sights? Adan's boots reverberated off the old floorboards as he headed for the hallway. This place felt…familiar. Not like he'd been here before, but it was the kind of place he'd take up as a safe house. Middle of nowhere, but close enough to town to switch out vehicles or make a run for the mountains. "There's a shed out back. Could be where Burgess is storing the ATV he took from his mother's house."

"Then where is he?" she asked.

Good question. Adan scanned a small four-piece bathroom—dated and gross as hell—then moved into one of the bedrooms. The first one was empty of furniture, but not the second. A mattress sat diagonal in the room, turned just right to keep an eye on the door and the window at the same time. A few chips bags and granola bar wrappers had been piled in one corner. Recent, from what Adan could tell. Another bathroom attached at the back, and he quickly cleared the room. Contact lens case with a tipped-over bottle of solution, toothbrush and a travel-size toothpaste, men's deodorant. "Whoever's been staying here planned to stick around for a while."

But the house was empty. He wasn't sure that was a good thing or a bad thing.

Isla's clean scent tickled the back of his throat as she came into the room behind him. She tossed a black duffel bag at his feet. "I found this in the closet on one of the shelves. Pushed back far enough to make it hard to reach."

Crouching, Adan felt the tightness running the length of Isla's neck and shoulders influence his own. He unzipped the bag and ripped it open wider. Hell. Something along the lines of disappointment and fury rocked through him.

"What is it?" She tried to get a better look by coming closer.

"It's a go bag." He pulled a banded stack of cash—totaling probably more than ten thousand dollars—from the depths and set it on the tile floor beside the bag. "Operatives and soldiers like to have supplies and necessities ready to go in case something goes wrong. Clothes, too." Adan tugged a T-shirt free, his fingers clenching in the material. This wasn't Layton Burgess's bag. He handed it off. Waiting for Isla's reaction.

Confusion deepened the two ridges on the inner edges of her eyebrows. Holstering her weapon, she fisted the fabric as though testing its feel for herself. "I don't understand. This is… This is Clint's shirt. I bought him this shirt on our first date to a rock concert. It was his favorite. Move." She dropped to one knee and pulled the bag's contents free. A gun, a box of ammunition, another shirt. And a photo.

Isla froze, staring down at the opaque faces. Unmoving, hardly breathing. Tears glittered in her eyes, and he knew there was nothing he could say, nothing he could do to ease the torrential storm hardening her from the inside. "How is this possible?"

He didn't have to see the picture to know whose smiles had been captured in the still. "Clint must've bought this place. He must've—"

"No." She raised her gaze to his. "This is wrong. He wouldn't have done this behind my back. He would've told me if he'd bought a house in the middle of the desert." A sob escaped up her chest, and Isla shoved to her feet. She backed out of the bathroom, her guard dissolved. She was on the edge and ready to shatter. Every breath seemed harder than the last, louder and gasping. "Somebody put this here. Somebody is using his death to lead us on a wild goose chase . I need some air."

Adan followed after her. He couldn't let her leave. Not until they were sure there wasn't anyone waiting for them to walk through the door. "Isla, stop. You can't go out there."

She retraced her steps and reached for the doorknob.

He wrapped both arms around her and hauled her

off her feet, turning his back to the door. The damn thing hinged open.

Burning ripped through his arm. The momentum of the bullet pitched him around. His grip fell from around Isla. He hit the ground. He slammed head-first into one of the kitchen counters.

Only Isla's scream echoed through his head. "Adan!"

Chapter Six

The door slammed back against the wall.

Wind ripped through the house and brought with it an extra dose of exposure. Adan was bleeding out. Unmoving. Unconscious. And right in the middle of the floor.

"Adan!" Both sides of her training kicked in. She could either stop the bleeding or make sure the shooter didn't come through that door to kill her. But she didn't really have a choice.

Isla holstered her weapon. She tried to recall what Clint had taught her in case she ever found herself under fire. In a town smaller than most neighborhoods, she hadn't ever thought she'd need that particular advice. She clenched onto Adan's shoulders and dug her heels into the floor.

A second bullet ripped past her ear.

A yip of a scream escaped past her lips. She fell back on her behind, still clutching Adan. The shooter was still out there. Fear and adrenaline combined into a volatile cocktail. She had to get Adan out of the line of sight, but any move she made only made her a better target.

"Adan, I can't do this by myself. Wake up." Isla leveraged her heels into the buckling floorboards a second time and heaved with everything she had. It wasn't enough. He was too heavy. There was no way she could move him herself. She dropped back with another failed attempt. What had Clint told her? Stay away from windows. Close all the doors. Fear crested again. Closing that door meant going back into the line of fire. She gauged the amount of blood soaking through Adan's T-shirt. "Okay."

Her attention locked on the swinging door. If Adan hadn't hauled her back, she would be the one on the floor. That was the third time he'd stepped between her a bullet. She owed him this. She owed him her life. And Mazi… She couldn't think about her daughter right now. The outcome would paralyze her into doing nothing, and Adan needed help. Now.

She could do this. Isla repositioned her legs beneath her and lunged.

The sound of a third shot cracked off the mountains after the bullet skimmed across the back of her skull. Searing pain burned along her scalp as she hit the floor. The impact knocked the air from her chest, but she couldn't lie there. She had to get to that door. Her pant leg caught on a loose nail as she stretched one hand toward the opening. She was still too far away to reach it. She tugged at her pants.

Seconds ticked by.

It wouldn't take the shooter long to reload.

Isla pressed her toes into the floor to give herself a little bit of extra length, but it was no use. The tip of her middle finger skimmed the old wood. She pulled at her pants again. Where had the department sourced these damn slacks? A lab that worked with spider silk?

A flash of light—like a shortened version of Morse code—crossed her vision. This was it. This was where Adan's personal mission failed. This was where Mazi lost the only parent she had left. Her jaw ached under the pressure of her back teeth. "No."

She latched on to Adan's left ankle and unsheathed the knife she knew he'd carried there since he'd come back from his first tour. Old habits died hard. With a single swipe, she cut her pant leg loose and vaulted off the floor.

The fourth bullet didn't miss its mark.

The force of impact pushed her back. She stumbled against the solitary recliner in the living room. Her knees gave out from the sheer agony tearing through her arm. The pain came fast and refused to let up. She clamped pressure with her other hand. She'd gotten out of the shooter's line of sight. Rushing forward, she kicked the door closed.

But now she had another problem.

Blood seeped through her fingers. It wouldn't take long for the shooter to come check to see if they were dead. Given the distance she'd gauged to that tell-tale glint of light, maybe a couple minutes. Not long enough to clean up two bullet wounds. Her heart threatened to give out right there; it could barely stay in her chest. "Hang on, Adan. I'm here. Okay? Just hang on."

She automatically dropped below the windows at the front of the house to stay out of sight. Practically crawling over Adan, she headed for the cabinet beneath the sink. It was a long shot, but it was the only one she had. She'd been an EMT going on twenty years. She always carried gear in case of an emergency, but running out to the trunk of the car wasn't an option right then. The cabinet stuck as she wrenched it open. Paint dislodged from the griminess, but low and behold, a first aid kit had been left behind. Actually, there was hardly any dust on it, and it wasn't the typical household kit she'd expected. No, this one was one of those mobilized rescue kits. Like whoever had owned this place knew she'd need it.

She hauled an oversize gray case free with her uninjured hand.

She didn't have time to think about that, about what they'd found in that duffel bag or who this house belonged to. Adan. She had to get to Adan. Seconds ticked off at the back of her head. Dragging the kit across the floor, she angled her knees on either side and popped it open. She couldn't help Adan without helping herself first.

The back of her arm was bleeding, too. The bullet had gone straight through. That would be the worst wound. She wasn't a doctor. She couldn't remove any bullets anyway. Her job as an EMT consisted of keeping people alive until they could get to the hospital. She pulled a length of rolled gauze from the kit and looped it around her arm as tightly as she could. It wasn't much, but it would have to work for a couple of minutes. Biting down on one end, she tied the gauze with her other hand.

Blinding white light ignited behind her eyes, and the world threatened to tip on its axis. No. She had to stay awake. She had to get Adan out of here. Clint's mantra slipped from her lips as her vision cleared. It had been the last two words he'd said to her before he left for Morocco. "Stay strong."

She'd stopped the bleeding enough to get her bearings. The kit scratched up the old floors as she dragged it closer to Adan. She wasn't sure where he'd been hit, but from the amount of blood on the floor, she could certify it was more than a flesh wound. "Come on, Adan. You can do this."

Isla put every last ounce of energy into flipping him onto his back. It took longer and more muscle than she expected, but he'd always been stubborn as a brick wall. Even when he was conscious. Blood gushed from the wound. There was no exit wound. The bullet was still in his shoulder. Not fatal if she could patch him until they could get medical attention.

A low rhythm registered through the hard pound of her heart behind her ears.

Footsteps. From the front porch.

The shooter was coming.

"I could really use your help, Sergeant." Out of the two options—stay and fight or drag Adan out of here— her training said to get the civilian out of the line of danger. She couldn't face off with a military-trained sniper with Adan caught in the middle. They had to go.

An outline shifted across one of the front windows.

She was out of time.

Isla fisted his collar with her uninjured hand and dragged him a couple inches toward the hallway. She'd noted another exit through the garage when they'd first searched the house. If she could get him there—

The door slammed open.

Too late.

Isla dropped her hold on Adan and reached to unholster her weapon.

"Make another move and you'll end up like my friend here, Officer Vachs." Shadow hid half of Layton Burgess's face, but she'd recognized him from his driver's license photo. His voice, broken and dry, sounded too harsh. Like the man had been yelling for hours with no one to hear him. Bulky muscle matched that of Clint and Adan. A war machine used for violence and duty. "Did he send you to kill me?"

"What?" She didn't understand. Every instinct she owned ordered her to follow through with un-holstering her weapon—to protect herself, to pro-tect Adan, to prevent another body from dropping in this investigation—but she had no doubt. Burgess would put her down as easily, if not more, as he'd put down Adan from hundreds of yards away. "N-no-body sent me. I'm with the Battle Mountain police. We got an anonymous tip your vehicle was spotted in this location—"

Layton Burgess unholstered a pistol and loaded a round into the gun barrel before taking aim straight between her eyes. He closed the distance between them, forcing Isla back until she hit a wall in the kitchen. Fury and exhaustion contorted his features. Sweat slipped from his chin and landed on the top of her boot. "Don't lie to me! Did Clint send you to kill me?"

Shock sucker punched her as though Burgess had physically struck her, and the result was more painful than two bullets in the span of two months. Her mouth worked to form the words. Two small words she'd never said in her life. Not even to her-self. "Clint's dead."

A crooked smile stretched Burgess's lacerated, dry lips. How long had he been out here? From the look of the skin around his tan collar, two days, maybe three. Before his mother had been tortured and killed. On the run? Burgess took a step back, that smile still in place, and lowered his pistol. He moved as gracefully as a predator, half turning away, but keeping his eye on her in case she decided to pull her weapon. "Yeah. That's what he'd want us to think, wouldn't he?"

"I don't know what that means." Movement agitated her already-stressed-out nervous system as Adan rolled onto his back. In her next breath, he was getting to his feet. How was that passible? She kept her attention on Burgess, doing everything she could not to give away Adan's recovery. He was alive. They were going to make it out of this.

Adan took a single step forward.

Burgess raised his weapon directly at Adan without even looking, his dark gaze locked on her. "It means your husband is the one killing off soldiers in my unit, but now I have something he wants."

ADAN DIDN'T GIVE Burgess a second chance.

He latched on to the soldier's wrist with his injured hand and tore the gun from Burgess's grip. The gun hit the floor, out of reach. Just as Burgess turned to shake him off, Adan launched his fist into the man's face. The bullet ripped deeper into the deep tissues of his shoulder, and a scream escaped his control. Momentum shoved the security operator into the wall beside Isla, and she ducked out of the way just in time. Adan took another shot with his nondominant arm, but Burgess dodged.

A wide swing aimed straight for his face. Adan balanced back on his heels to avoid the hit. It took him only a second to regain control. He shoved Burgess into the wall a second time. Another wave of agony almost put him down. The drywall cracked and splintered from the weight as Adan slammed his elbow into the side of Burgess's face.

"Watch out!" Isla's warning came too late.

The swish of a blade was drowned by stinging pain slashing across his torso. Burgess followed it up with a kick centered to Adan's chest. He fell back, collapsing into the back of the recliner in the living room. The jolt shifted the bullet in his shoulder, but he didn't have the time to level out. He grabbed a lamp that had been knocked down from the side table in the middle of the fight and swung at the soldier's head as hard as he could.

Burgess fell.

Hell. Adrenaline drained fast. Adan dropped to one knee beside Burgess's body.

"Is he dead?" Isla took a step forward, clutching her gun with both hands as though holding on to it brought some comfort. He didn't blame her.

Burgess's back rose and fell in even rhythms.

"No." Adan clamped a hand over his shoulder. In a couple of minutes the swelling would make it impossible to use it at all. Isla rushed to help him stand, taking his weight into her hip. She was hard and soft in all the right places. Although if he collapsed, he'd take her down with him. "Good news. We found Burgess. Bad news. I think he wants to kill us."

She directed him to the kitchen table now shoved up against one of the cabinets. "Sit. Don't move. I need to take a look at that wound as long as he's unconscious and call for backup."

It wasn't Burgess he was worried about. Adan kept tabs on anything usual through the front window. Burgess wasn't a trained sniper. He'd obviously gotten hold of a rifle, but he'd missed Adan's chest. Then again, the man had somehow settled on the idea Clint had sent Adan and Isla out to kill him. Isla passed in front of him as she hauled a massive first aid kit from the floor and dropped it on the table with a thud. She unhitched her radio from her belt and hit the call button three times, but the short-wave radio wasn't responding. He saw red lines dripping down her arm. He pulled her in front of him to get a better look. "You're shot. How bad?"

She set down the radio, turning her attention to him. "Better than you. You're still carrying a bullet, and the longer it's in there, the more damage it'll cause." She was putting his needs in front of her own. Once a first responder, always a first responder. But the thought of her taking another bullet raised his protectiveness to an entirely new level.

"Now hold still," she said. "The bullet is pressing out the front of your shoulder. The only way to stop the bleeding is to get it out." She drew a scalpel from the kit. "And it's going to hurt."

They didn't have time to play doctor.

Adan pushed to his feet. In less than three steps, he flipped Burgess onto his back and clutched the man's jaw with his good hand. "Wake up, Burgess."

"What are you doing?" Isla followed him with a bottle of disinfectant and the scalpel. "You've got a bullet lodged in your shoulder."

"He shot you." Fire bolted through his system. It was one thing to take a shot at him, but Adan had promised himself he wouldn't let anything happen to her. And he was still failing. "I don't know about you, but I take offense at someone coming after the people I love." He tapped Burgess's face with the back of his hand. "Come on, big boy. Rise and shine. There you go."

Burgess groaned, blinking up at him. "Sergeant? What—"

"That's right." Adan fisted the soldier's T-shirt collar and hefted the man's upper body off the floor. "That's the third time someone has taken a shot at Isla, and I'm in no mood for more games. Now, I know you're not the shooter. You don't have the skills, but I think you know who's killing off our unit. Why don't you take this opportunity to unburden yourself before I have you court-martialed."

Burgess's gaze went to Isla, and a rising flood of heat burned through Adan.

"Adan." There was that warning again. As though Isla could sense the danger the man who'd shot her was in. She was an officer of the law, sworn to uphold it. Would she arrest him if his desperation to protect her went too far?

He brought Burgess closer. "Don't you look at her. Don't even think you get my permission to utter her name." His voice dipped an octave of its own accord. "Tell me who's behind these shootings. Who killed Moore and White, who came after me three months ago and who is gunning for Isla now? Who are you running from?"

"Clint," Burgess said.

"You're lying." He nearly dropped Burgess to the floor. "Clint's been dead a year. I escorted his body back to the States myself. I watched them put him in the ground right here in Battle Mountain. I watched his wife and his daughter say goodbye to a good man."

Isla shifted in his peripheral vision.

"You don't get it, do you?" Burgess blinked in rapid succession. "It's not just him. It's all of them. The whole unit. This place… This was just one of their drop locations. That's why I came here. I wanted proof."

Confusion ricocheted to connect the dots. Adan's arm was getting tired of holding the soldier in place. "Proof of what?"

"Of their smuggling ring." Burgess shook his

head. "Clint, Moore, White. All of them. I saw it go down in Morocco, right before that big meeting to unload the choppers. They caught me. Clint offered to bring me into the operation, but I told him I didn't want anything to do with it. They were going to kill me, but the next thing I know, the Moroccans are there, and the deal's going south. I got out of there as fast as I could. I swear I'm telling the truth."

"Smuggling what?" Adan would've been added to that list of dead if he hadn't escaped with a bullet for a souvenir.

"Like you didn't already know about the drugs." Burgess answered as if it were that obvious, but a fissure of uncertainty was still cutting through Adan. Clint wouldn't have been involved in a smuggling operation. He wouldn't have been trying to bring drugs into the States from the Middle East.

"You're lying." Isla crossed the room in a fury of thunder and anger. She tried to get to Burgess around Adan, but he straightened to hold her off. She clawed at Burgess on the floor until Adan managed to force her back. "Who the hell do you think you are? My husband was a good man. He was an honest man. He loved his country, and he died to protect it, you son of a bitch. I'm not going to let you ruin his reputation." She turned pleading eyes to Adan. "He's lying. Clint never would've—"

"I know." He secured his good arm around her, holding her against his chest. His frame nearly engulfed hers, but she fit so perfectly at the same time. Adan notched her chin higher, and she locked watery eyes on him. "But beating this guy senseless isn't going to give us any answers, and it sure won't help your position in the department."

She rolled her lips between her teeth. "Fine, but I'm not going to stand here and listen to this garbage."

He let her out of his hold, and she headed for the back bedrooms. His nervous system protested against having her out of sight, but Isla needed space. A lot of space.

"All right. Say I believe you. Moore, White, Clint— they were smuggling drugs into the States. Why set up shop in Battle Mountain?" Adan turned back to Burgess.

"Because of her." Burgess nodded in Isla's direction. "Clint couldn't stand to be away from her and his kid. He bought this place just far enough out of town so she wouldn't suspect, but he could still keep an eye on the operation. The other guys, they'd stay here and make sure everything went smoothly with the deals. Right up until they were pumped full of lead." Burgess dropped his attention to the floor. "Guess I don't have to worry about them anymore. Thanks to you."

"You think I'm the one cleaning up." It made sense. Adan had the record and the ties to put him behind the scope. He offered Burgess his hand. "Hate to break it to you, Burgess. I haven't touched my rifle in a year. But for what it's worth, I'm sorry about your mother. She didn't deserve to go out like that."

Burgess stared at Adan's hand like he was some kind of creature from the black lagoon. "You think that because you're telling me you didn't do it, I trust you, Sergeant? How do I know all this isn't some kind of ploy to get in my head?"

"Because I don't need both my arms to add you to the list of dead men, Burgess," he said. "If I'd wanted you dead, I would've taken you out first."

"All right. Fine." Burgess shoved to his feet without help. "If you're not the one picking our unit off one by one, then who is, and what the hell do they want?"

"I imagine whoever it is they're covering their tracks. Operation must not be going too well if they're tying up loose ends. First Moore. Then White. Shooter came after me. He must've thought Clint had read me in." His instincts battled to accept that truth. Isla was right. Clint wouldn't have gotten involved in a smuggling ring, but with the evidence they'd pulled out of that duffel bag combined with this place… What other choice did he have but to acknowledge Clint was involved? Adan motioned to Burgess. "You witnessed one of their deals, so you're high on their priority list. That's why he went after your mother. Must've thought she'd know where you were."

But that still didn't explain why the shooter had come after Isla. She didn't have anything to do with this. He scanned the front of the house through the window in the living room.

A glint of light brought his attention to the first hill leading into the mountain.

"Get down!" Adan hit the floor as the bullet shattered the window. Glass rained down around him and sliced down his arms and the back of his neck.

Burgess hit the floor.

Chapter Seven

The gunshot echoed off the mountains.

Isla turned back to the house. She'd needed distance—space—to figure this out, and she couldn't do it confined to a house that was starting to look like her husband's secret. Now, she realized, she'd only put them in danger by leaving. "Adan."

The all-too-familiar crack of the bullet threatened to bring back memories of pain and blood and fear, but in that moment she could think only about the man who'd saved her life. She pumped her legs hard until they burned.

Another crack split the empty silence of the desert.

The dirt at her feet exploded.

It took everything she had to fight the momentum. She pulled to a stop, exposed out in the open. Just like the shooter wanted. The house and Adan—safety itself—were only a few more yards in front of her. She could make a run for it, but something told her this marksman wouldn't miss like Layton Burgess had. That he'd hit his target at least once before.

"Adan?" Tremors shook through her hands as she raised them above her head in surrender. She studied the ridge, trying to find any anomalies that would give her an idea of where the shooter had set up position. But the sun was in her eyes, she didn't know this area and she wasn't a trained sniper. She had no idea what to look for or who they were up against. All she had was her training and her instincts. Right now they were telling her that if she didn't make it to that house, she wasn't making it out alive at all. Isla closed her eyes and tried to summon a small amount of courage that had fled over the past hour.

She moved toward the house.

A second bullet impacted at her feet.

An involuntary yip rushed past her lips, and she took two more steps back. Away from Adan and answers and the chance to pick up Mazi from school. Air stalled in her lungs. Scrub brush scratched against her slacks as she retreated. Out here, she was nothing more than a target. But maybe in these mountains she'd have a chance. She kept moving backward. "What do you want from me!"

Her question bounced off the rolling hills standing guard to the jagged monster claws of rock behind them. Clouds shifted overhead, and for a brief moment, the sun relented. The shooter would have a clearer view of her now, but when the clouds parted again, she could run for it. She could hide until he gave up. These mountains stretched for miles. No way he'd be able to search them all on his own.

Her breathing drowned out the whistle of wind, then hitched as her heels angled higher than her toes. Her calves burned as she hiked backward up the first rolling hill. The house seemed so far away now, yet still so close. Within reach. She scanned the landscape to get some kind of bearing, but it was no use. She was out of her league here.

And Adan… Adan could be bleeding out. Could've taken another bullet. He'd already lost so much blood. Not only that but she'd left him with a paranoid soldier convinced they'd been sent to kill him. Her chin wobbled with held-in tears. She wouldn't break. For her own sake. For Adan's.

Her heel caught on a rock. Isla lost her balance and hit the ground. Gravity pulled her down the opposite side of the hill, and the house vanished from sight. Dirt and thorns stabbed into her already wounded arm as she rolled. Twice. Three times. Her stomach vaulted into her throat as she came to a stop staring up at the prettiest sky she'd ever seen.

The afternoon sun was low enough to cast shade where she'd ended up, which meant… *"You can't see me here."*

The shooter wouldn't have a good line of sight. A small thrill of victory helped her get to her feet. She spit out the dirt caked inside her mouth and tested her wound. A different kind of pain lanced through her. Aching, exhausted pain, but she couldn't stay here. Every second she fought her reality, the faster the shooter would find her. She peeled bloody gauze from her wound. The makeshift tourniquet had held. She wouldn't bleed out. Yet. Clamping her hand over the hole in her arm, she stumbled along the base of the hill. Adan couldn't get to her here. Not with a shooter on the loose. She was on her own,

She'd never been much of an outdoorsy person. The first—and last—time Clint had taken her camping had ended in disaster. Adan had been on that trip. While her husband had finally given up hope to teach her how to start a primitive fire, Adan had stuck with her. He'd been patient and kept his calm. It had taken hours, and she'd complained the entire time. Isla slowed as the memory solidified without permission. Seemed even then he'd been too stubborn to recognize a lost cause, but in the end, she'd learned how to set that fire. His unending patience was just one of the things she'd appreciated about him.

A twig snapped from behind her.

Isla didn't have the chance to turn around to defend herself.

Heavy muscle tackled her to the ground. Another mouthful of dirt worked down her throat as she tried to claw out from beneath the mass fighting to get her arms behind her back. Her arm screamed for relief under the weight. "Get off me!"

She managed to wiggle free with a strong strike

from her elbow and shot to her feet. Turning to gauge her attacker, she backed away quickly as a Viking of a man advanced. Sun glimmered off his cleanly shaven head. Light-colored eyes narrowed in on her. She went for her gun and froze. Her gun. It was gone. She searched the ground around her feet. It must've come free during her fall, and she hadn't noticed. Isla bent to pick up a good-sized rock and swung it at her attacker instead. She slammed it into the side of his head. The force twisted his face away from her, but he didn't go down. Shock held her in place for a split second before Isla dropped the rock, turned and ran.

He was three times her size, but she was fast. She darted along the base of the hill she'd fallen behind, toward a larger swell. Heavy footprints stomped behind her. The Viking was closing in. She risked a glance over her shoulder. Another outline materialized off to her left, although she wasn't going to take the time to memorize his face. Fear drilled straight to her core. She was outnumbered and outgunned with nothing but miles of mountains and desert to finish her off.

She didn't have a choice. She had to risk it.

Isla put every last ounce of energy into her legs as she climbed the next rise. Another bullet—she'd lost count of how many—shot dirt up her side, but she didn't stop. They hadn't killed her yet, which meant they needed her for something. Just like they'd needed Gail Oines.

A third figure stepped into her path up ahead as though he'd been waiting for her all along.

She skidded to a stop short of a collection of Joshua trees. The two men behind her sauntered closer. She'd been herded like cattle. The Viking bared his teeth in an evil attempt at a smile, just as a sheepdog might do if one of its charges stepped out of line. "What do you want?"

"Not much." The second man rounded behind her. Trying to keep her distracted? Off-balance? It was working. If the man who'd tackled her was a Viking, this one would be his exact opposite in every way but size. Dark hair, dark eyes, sun-tanned skin. Only this one, she knew. His photo was hanging on the wall she'd dedicated to Clint and the men and women he'd served with. His leather jacket was too out of place in the middle of the desert. She couldn't imagine he was comfortable in it. Then again, why did she care? "Just tell us where the shipment your husband stole from us is, and we'll leave you and this hellhole behind."

"Fischer?" His name snapped into place. He'd visited her and Clint's home during one of their summer barbecues for the unit. He'd been in the same room with her daughter. He'd helped her carry out fresh drinks, for crying out loud. She'd liked him. All of them. And they were the ones who wanted her dead? Isla tried to keep all three men in sight, but they kept moving around. Disorienting her. "Why are you doing this?"

"Come on, Isla. Don't pretend you didn't know this day was coming." Fischer took a step forward, rubbing one fist into his opposite hand. Too soon, he was right in front of her. He reached out, gripping her chin in his hand. "I've always liked you, but as much as I'd hate to have to do something to this pretty little face, I've got my orders."

She batted away his hand and wrenched free of his hold. "I don't know what shipment you're talking about. I don't know what you want from me."

"You could be telling the truth." Fischer said. "Or maybe you're as good a liar as Clint. Why don't we see what Mazi says?"

"What?" No. No, no, no, no. They didn't have Mazi. It was just another way to get inside her head, make her tell them something she didn't know. But convincing her heart this was all some kind of manipulation would take more than assumptions. She searched her brain for some way out of this. She could run for it, make them chase her instead of them focusing on Mazi, but she couldn't leave her daughter to fend for herself.

Isla memorized the men's positions around her. None of them was carrying a rifle, which meant there was most likely a fourth man. The shooter who'd put a bullet in her side and through Adan's shoulder two months ago. The one who'd tried to kill her again last night. Was he the one who had Mazi? Isla stepped into Fischer as fear dissipated. In its place, rage. It wasn't enough she'd lost Clint. They'd come after her family. "What did you do with my daughter?"

"You didn't think we would lure you all the way out here without a little insurance policy, did you?" Fischer's half-cocked smile only lasted a moment.

Right before she launched her fist into his face.

Fischer fell back, clutching his jaw. The other two men rushed forward, but she wouldn't stop. She hit Fischer again, and a third time. Blood spattered across the back of her hand and onto her face. She set her elbow back for another strike. "Where is she?"

Pain arced through the back of her head.

And the world tipped on its axis.

"DON'T YOU DARE die on me." Adan overlaid one hand with the other and did another round of chest compressions. "Come on, Burgess. Who's behind this? Who's coming after Isla? Tell me!"

It was no use.

He'd been trying to revive the security operator for a good three minutes. He didn't have to be an EMT to accept the truth. Layton Burgess only stared up at the ceiling, a permanent expression of shock and sadness etched onto his face. Like his mother.

Adan fell back, one leg hiked over Burgess's. Blood gushed from his shoulder. He pressed his bloodied palm into the center to try to stop the bleeding. "Damn it."

Four soldiers from his unit. Gunned down. And for what? Some kind of drug operation Clint had been involved in before his death? His gut said it was all a lie, but what other explanation was there? This place, Clint's go bag shoved into a closet—it was starting to look just as Burgess had said.

His heart pounded hard. The faster it beat, the sooner he'd bleed out. He had to keep his calm, but the shooter was still out there. And Isla… Oh, hell. She'd stormed to the back of the house while he'd questioned Burgess. Then the shot had come through the window. Everything had happened so fast he hadn't had time to think about where she'd gone. "Isla?"

Adan got to his feet. No answer. Instinct and a heavy dose of protectiveness pushed the pain tearing through his shoulder to the back of his mind. He'd trained to compartmentalize. Sooner or later his body would give out, but not before he found Isla.

He ripped through the house. She wasn't here. Her patrol vehicle was still parked out front. That left the back door, but why would she have gone out the back after the shot?

Unless she'd gone to confront the shooter herself.

"Damn it, woman." He shouldered through the back door and out into the open. The sun was getting lower, but there was still enough light to discern the tracks in the dirt. One set led a few yards out. Smaller. Maybe size seven, size eight. Narrow. Most definitely Isla's. He followed along from a few feet away until they seemed to pool together. Ridges were lost, the pattern on the bottom of her boots no longer clean. She'd turned back toward the house. Then stopped.

A clump of dirt—so out of place among the flat, cracked land around the property—claimed his attention. Adan bent down, one hand still over his shoulder. He repositioned himself to get a better view. And saw the expended bullet inside.

A .30 caliber round.

Adan shoved to stand. "Isla!"

Her name bounced off the high cliff faces of the mountains and through the canyons carved into them. Still no answer. There were a couple more treads behind the initial collection, but the weight distribution was heavier in the heels. Like she'd been walking backward. He followed the tracks to another clump of dirt. Collecting a second bullet, he weighed them both in his hand as understanding bled into focus. "Son of a bitch."

The shooter had forced her away from the house.

She was out here. Vulnerable, alone, with no idea of what she was up against. Adan jogged to the ridge where her tracks ended. There were different impressions here. Skids down the hill. She'd fallen. Digging his heels in, he slid down on his side. A dark outline stood out among the colorless shadows encroaching on this side of the rise. A Glock 22. The same gun Isla carried. He hit the button for the magazine release. Full clip. It must've come loose after her fall, but that didn't explain—

A second set of treads mixed with hers. Larger. Heavier. If he didn't know any better, he'd say military, from the pattern. A close match to Adan's. Both sets of footprints headed along the bottom of the hill. Someone had chased her. Someone big. He holstered her weapon at the small of his back and jogged to follow the trail. She couldn't have been gone long. Five, ten minutes. She was still out here. She was still alive. He had to believe that. "I'm coming, Isla. Just hang on."

The pain in his arm pierced through his focus. Air crushed from his chest at the impact. Webs of black spidered at the edges of his vision, but he wasn't going to stop. Not until he found her. He picked up the pace. He wasn't going to fail her like he failed Clint. She deserved better than that, and Mazi deserved to grow up with at least one parent.

Isla had put everyone else in her life ahead of her. Clint, the unit, Mazi, even the men and women she'd worked beside in fire and rescue. She was the most unselfish, family-oriented person he'd ever known. She'd gone out of her way to look after everyone, to save lives and bring people together. Her compassion, sincerity and patience rivaled Mother Teresa's herself, and it physically pained him to think of the world without her in it. She needed someone to fight for her. He needed to fight for her.

The tracks went from clear impressions to a jumble of movement and confusion. He couldn't tell Isla's apart from the mass, but one thing was clear. Blood. A few drops in the dirt, and when his vision adjusted more to the encroaching darkness, he spied a spatter on the Joshua tree a couple feet away. His gut clenched. Isla's? Two other sets of footprints brought the count up to three attackers. Against one woman. He traced the pattern of blood down the tree with one hand. "Why make it a fair fight?"

A wave of dizziness clocked him hard. The tree's spindles cut into his hand as he tried to keep his feet under him. As for where the bastards were now, Adan couldn't tell. Two of the larger sets had headed into a maze of scrub brush while the third had continued along the base of the hill. No sign of Isla. If Burgess had been telling the truth, soldiers from his own damn unit were responsible, which meant they knew of his and Isla's connection. They'd planned for him to come out here and had split up to slow him down.

No drag marks. Someone had carried Isla out of here. Logic demanded he follow the two sets of tracks deeper into the mountains, but his gut had him tracking the single set along the hill. He picked up the pace. They hadn't killed her. The shooter and whoever else he'd brought with him wanted her for something. He just had to find out what. Before it was too late.

Sweat built at the back of his collar despite the dropping temperatures. It was mid-November in one of the coldest states in America. Temperatures wouldn't reach above thirty overnight. He stumbled into the side of the hill. His vision went dark, and it took everything he had to breathe through the rush of dragging lethargy closing in on his head. He'd lost too much blood. His body was shutting down. "Not an option, Sergeant. Move."

Adan worked to stand. One knee collapsed out from underneath him. He'd survived two tours in the Middle East, losing his best friend, being shut out by the only people he loved, a bullet to the shoulder two months ago and another attempt last night. He'd survive this. For Isla. For Mazi.

You gotta protect them. Promise me, Sarge. They'll need you. Promise me. Clint's voice tendrilled through the mess of pain and emotion. He could still feel the grip his best friend had had on his hand, as though Clint couldn't let go until he knew his girls were taken care of. Now Adan understood why. Adan had told him everything would be fine, that he was going to make it, but they'd both known the truth. The bullet had found its mark. According to Burgess, Clint had gotten himself embroiled in a smuggling operation. Any number of threats could've turned his way, and he'd wanted his family protected. Insurance. That was what Adan was. Peace of mind. A surge of clarity got him to his feet. He'd given his word that day in Morocco, and he had no intention of backing out now. He'd find Isla. He'd bring her home to her daughter, and he'd end this. "I promise."

"I told him you wouldn't fall for the bait," a voice said from behind. Familiar. One he'd heard a dozen times over comms and in the barracks. "Damn, Sarge. You don't look so good."

Adan faced off with Brett Fischer, another of the men from his unit. The joint fire support specialist had been assigned to their team to provide artillery expertise. It had been Fischer's job to assess the threat of an ambush that day in Morocco. If Adan wasn't so determined to take the blame for Clint's death, Fischer would be at the front of the line. He pulled back his shoulder, ignoring the bite of metal digging into tendon and muscle. At six-four, his teammate and he were evenly matched. However, there really was only way to test that theory. "Figured you'd be wrapped up in this, Fischer. You always were looking for a payday."

"Careful, Sarge, that almost makes it sound like you don't like me." Fischer cocked his head to one side, and Adan got a full view of a dried blood and swelling across his face.

The blood back at the patch of Joshua trees. It

wasn't Isla's. She'd fought back. Pretty well from the look of it, too.

"That's one way of putting it. I like what you've done to your face. I take it your abduction didn't go as planned." He couldn't help but smile, but as Fischer took a step closer, every muscle in his body tightened in battle-ready defense. Fischer hadn't come out here to slow him down. He'd come to stop him. Adan had gotten too close. "Where is she?"

"Which one?" Fischer asked. "They kind of look alike, don't you think?"

A low ringing filtered in his ears. Mazi. His heart threatened to beat straight out of his chest. "You went after the girl."

"Like I told Isla, we needed our own insurance. At least until she tells us where Clint hid the shipment he stole from us." Fischer pressed one fist into his opposite palm. "Say, you wouldn't happen to know the location, would you? It had sure save us from having to tear this town apart. Not to mention the man's wife and daughter."

"Hurt either of them, and it'll be the last thing you do," he said.

Fischer's laugh punctured through the night. The distinct unsheathing of a blade registered. "How are you going to do anything for them, Sarge, if you're dead?"

Chapter Eight

Isla pulled her chin away from her chest. Her head fell back between her raised arms. What... Where was she? She'd been running from...men. Three men. One had knocked her out from behind. Fischer's face materialized in her mind. She'd clocked him pretty good. Served him right.

Her head cleared with every inhale of crisp night air. The sun had settled completely, and a vast array of stars that had amazed her the first night she and Mazi had come here sparkled in dark, ribbony velvet. She was cold. Her feet dangled a few inches from the ground. She could barely make out the rope binding her wrists to a Joshua tree. The spindles scratched at her back and pricked at her exposed skin.

Fischer and his men had taken her uniform shirt and her shoes and socks, leaving her in nothing but slacks and her tank top.

This was wrong. All of it. She tried to use her weight to snap the branch they'd hung her on and jerked down. It wouldn't budge. Her head felt as though it was cracked in two. Considering the force they'd used to knock her out, she wouldn't be surprised to find she'd suffered a skull fracture trying to fight three soldiers at once. Then again, the chances of getting to a hospital for tests seemed a little unrealistic.

Movement cut through the night, but there was no sign of anyone. Had they just left her to die? The rest of her memory caught up. "Mazi?"

"Your daughter is safe, Officer Vachs. For now." A click registered. Then the soft glow of a match. Warm, orange light highlighted the face of a man a few feet away, as though he'd been there the entire time, watching her. The length of a rifle stood guard beside him on the large rock he'd taken up. Sooner than she wanted, the cigarette caught, and the matched died out. Casting her back into darkness.

It was unsettling. Knowing he could see her, but she couldn't see him. She swallowed back the dryness coating her throat. "She has nothing to do with this. Where is she?"

"Right where you left her. Whispering Pines Ranch." The speck of burning red shot upward as the shooter stood. "And she'll stay there, with the old woman watching over her, as long as you cooperate. If you don't... Well, that's another conversation we'll have to have."

They didn't have Mazi.

A surge of relief urged her to relax, but seeing as

how she'd been strung up in the middle of the desert, now might not be a good time. The dusty sound of footprints grew louder. He'd closed the distance between them. Isla watched that cigarette, and another inhale brightened the man's face. This was the gunman who'd taken a shot at her two months ago, who'd tried to kill her again last night. She didn't understand how she knew, but her gut had filled in the blanks. He'd taken another shot not that long ago. Whom had he been targeting then? The answer was already there, waiting for her acceptance. "And Adan?"

"You have more important things to worry about other than the man who left you unprotected, Officer Vachs." The cigarette was discarded and snuffed out in the dirt. Only a sliver of moonlight peeked out from behind the clouds and outlined the man in front of her. "Like telling me where my boss's shipment is."

Isla tried to twist her wrists free from the rope. If she couldn't see the shooter out here in the dead of night, it stood to reason he couldn't see her. Right? "I already told Fischer before he and his merry band of jerks knocked me out. I don't know what you're talking about."

His low rumble of a laugh silenced the rustle of wind and insects. The shooter rounded behind her, and a whole new set of fears charged to the surface faced with the unknown. "Let me tell you about the man you married, Officer Vachs. Not the one who came home to you after tour, scooped you up in his arms, took you to bed the first chance he got and promised to stay with you forever. The real Clint Vachs."

Pressure built between her shoulder blades.

"The Clint I knew killed a lot of people. He lied to the soldiers in his unit. Men and women who trusted him to have their backs." The man-shaped shadow returned from its orbit around her and stopped dead ahead. "He convinced the people I work for he could get something for them, that we could make a lot of money together. He arranged the entire deal, and then without warning, he stole from us." The shooter stepped in closer. Calloused skin caught along her jaw and pushed her hair back behind one ear, and right then she realized he could see her. Every detail. Every move. "Now, I've been very patient, Isla, but you see, those people I just told you about are not. They want what they paid for, and it's up to me to get it to them."

Her fingers had gone numb from the weight of her body against the ropes. She twisted her wrists again, but there was no give. "The man you're talking about, the Clint you claim to know, doesn't exist. You're lying."

She read a hint of a smile on his face as another beam of moonlight cut through the night. A pattern of short facial hair and thick eyebrows emerged, but not enough to make an ID on the shooter if given the chance after tonight.

"You're still grieving. I understand, and I don't need to convince you of the truth." He took a step back and headed for the rock he'd evacuated a few minutes ago. Bending to collect something—she couldn't see what—he returned. "I just want what's mine. So tell me this, where would Clint hide something from you?"

"He wouldn't." Confidence entwined with her voice despite the agony tearing through her arm. The bullet wound had stopped bleeding as far as she could tell, but that might only be because her arms were elevated. "My husband had no reason to hide anything from me."

But he had. Clint's go bag had been in that house. Whether or not Layton Burgess had been telling the truth, her husband had been inside a house in the middle of the desert that supported a smuggling ring. He'd lied to her. But she wasn't going to give the son of a bitch who'd threatened her daughter the time of day.

"Oh, come now, Officer Vachs. We all have our secrets." A glint of metal drew her attention to the shooter's hand. He tossed the blade's sheath to the ground. "I'm sure you even have a few of your own. I've already had my men tear apart your home and search the house out here. I've got Fischer taking care of Adan right now, and a man watching Whispering Pines Ranch. So I want you to think really hard before you lie to me again. Where did Clint hide my shipment?"

Battle Mountain PD would protect Mazi. But taking care of Adan? What did that mean? He must've survived the shot that had had her rushing back to the house, but there was still the matter of the bullet in his shoulder. After two interferences to save her life, she knew he wouldn't stop fighting, even at the expense of his own life. Whatever Fischer had planned, it wouldn't work. Because despite all the things she'd hated about Adan after Clint's death, he was loyal above reproach. Committed, protective and sacrificing. He'd do whatever it took to find her, and he'd guard Mazi after he found Isla's body. "You underestimate him. Adan. I think you know it, too. I think that's why you're here with me, and you sent Fischer and those two other traitors after him. He wasn't part of your operation. You didn't want him to know about it. Because you're scared, and you should be. Fischer and your buddies? They're already dead, and you're out of time."

Hesitation thickened between them, but Isla had no doubts.

"Well, all right, then." The shooter latched on to one foot. A prick pierced the bottom of her heel. The blade. There were any number of veins and nerves in the bottom of the feet. Cutting them could cause permanent damage. If the shooter was military like

Clint and Adan and Fischer, he'd most likely done his research. He would've known she'd only become a BMPD officer in the past two months and that her former life revolved around saving lives. EMTs knew anatomy, just like their hospital counterparts. He was making a point, and he wanted her to know it. "Let's play a game while we wait, shall we? See how long it takes your soldier to find you before you bleed out."

He sliced into the bottom of her foot.

A whimper escaped her control, and Isla kicked out. She caught him in the center of the chest and shoved him back. Stinging pain rippled along her heel, distracting her long enough for him to get a hold of her other foot. Another cut lacerated the sensitive skin, and he backed off. The injuries triggered her heart rate to spike. Her fight-or-flight instinct kicked in, but she couldn't do either.

Isla dropped her head back, trying to get a better look at the ropes around her wrists. She couldn't feel them anymore. Her hands had gone numb, and a tingling sensation prickled down her arms. Gravity was doing its job, and with the cuts in the bottoms of her feet, it would exsanguinate her within the hour.

Reality weakened her confidence. What if she was wrong? What if Adan didn't come for her? Fear beaded sweat along the back of her neck despite the cold night. Mazi would be alone. The nightmares would start again. She'd have no one to love her as much as Isla did, and her daughter deserved that love.

She deserved everything Isla and Clint had worked for. A heaviness pulled at her last reserves of energy as her life force literally drained. "You don't have to do this. You can still let me go. Please. I don't know what Clint took from you, and I don't want to know, but I can help you find it."

"I think it's a little too late for that, Officer Vachs." The shooter threw his blade into the dirt. The tip embedded into the dry crust of the earth, and he took his position back on the rock to light another cigarette. A puff of smoke rose into the clear night sky. "Ticktock, ticktock."

ADAN SLAMMED HIS head into Fischer's face.

Isla would say he'd always had a thick skull.

He spread his hand over Fischer's eyes to block his view and rammed a fist into the bastard's head.

Fischer recovered fast, as they were trained to do. The soldier got in a descent right hook. Lightning struck behind Adan's eyes. Fischer went again and hit his mark.

With a third strike, Adan rammed his elbow down into the fire support's forearm as hard as he could and uppercutted with everything he had.

His attacker stumbled back. Adan shoved him down the rest of the way, and the son of a bitch hit the dirt. "That's for coming after Isla two months ago." Adan rocketed his boot into the soldier's rib cage. "That's for last night." He kicked again. "That's for hunting her down like an animal." Fisting the soldier's collar, Adan hauled his upper body off the ground, another fist cocked. Pain tendrilled through his shoulder, but he wasn't going to let it stop him. "Now tell me where she is."

Fischer let his head fall back, then turned his face to spit blood. "You think we were hard on her before? You haven't seen anything yet, Sergeant. It's not just about the shipment or her knowing where it is. There's always more where that came from. This is about Clint. This is about him betraying us. He got what was coming to him back in Morocco, but it's not enough. We're here to send a message. Screw with us, and you, your family, everyone you ever cared about suffers, too. Isla and Mazi? They're just the cherry on top."

"You killed Clint. It wasn't one of the Moroccans like the final report says." Adan released his hold, standing over Fischer. Every cell in his body wanted to make sure the specialist couldn't hurt Isla or Mazi ever again, but he didn't kill in cold blood and not without reason. It wasn't in his makeup. "That's why he wanted me to protect Isla and Mazi. He knew you'd come after them. He knew one of his own men had taken him out."

"I didn't pull the trigger, if that's what you're thinking, Sergeant." Fischer spat again, rolling onto his side before he shoved to his feet. "That honor went to someone else, but I may have had a hand in his final days. Just like I'll have a hand in yours."

Two more outlines stepped from the shadows.

"Did I forget to mention I brought along som friends?" Fischer asked.

Bills and Gurr—two other soldiers assigned in Morocco—took position behind and at an angle. He was surrounded. "The more the merrier."

Silence descended. Adan leveled off his breathing, his senses at high alert.

Bills—over six-four and two hundred and fifty pounds of Viking heritage—stepped in. He swung wide with his right. Adan caught Bills's wrist with one hand, angled the bastard down and positioned his other at the side of the soldier's head. Right into a rock. Lights out for Bills.

Gurr didn't waste any time. He swung a blade close to Adan's chin, and Adan barely managed to dodge.

Adan slammed his hand against the butt of the knife and stopped Gurr's advance. He struck with his opposite hand. Once. Twice. Gurr's head snapped back. Adan disarmed the soldier of the knife and wrapped his forearm around the man's neck. Dragging him along, Adan approached Fischer and kicked the bastard across the face before discarding Gurr at his feet. Fischer dropped. "Now, who wants to tell me where my girls are?"

The claim to Isla and Mazi came so naturally that he barely realized he'd said the words aloud. Groans filled the night in response. "Nobody?" Adan fought to catch his breath. Adrenaline was draining fast.

The pain in his shoulder had hit an all-time high, but he wasn't finished. He'd reached the end of his patience. "All right. Then you and I are going to take a field trip, Fischer."

He disarmed each man in turn, tossing a collection of pistols and blades into the desert. All but one. Fisting Fischer's collar, he dragged the operator behind him as he continued along the trail of tracks. He wasn't sure how far they'd gone, but there was no sign of Isla or Mazi.

"It's too late." Fischer's gargled words seeped past Adan's rage. "He already has her."

Adan slowed to a stop. Her. Not them. Did that mean Fischer's insinuation he'd taken Mazi had been a lie? Hope knotted in his gut. "Who has her?"

"It doesn't matter." Fischer attempted to shake his head, and his voice wore thin. "She doesn't have a chance against the people we work for. None of us do."

Adan dropped the soldier harder than he'd planned but didn't feel bad about it considering Fischer had abducted Isla and attempted to skewer Adan with his blade. He tapped the operator's face a little harder than necessary with aching fingers. "Tell me where she is, Fischer. Where did you take her?"

"To the tree." Fischer fell back into unconsciousness.

The tree? There weren't any trees out here. Not unless—

Dozens of spidery fingers reached into the sky in

every direction around him. Adan studied the closest. Joshua trees. All right. He'd play along. Fischer had said the tree. Could be one that stood out among the others. Size? He scanned the moonlit landscape and targeted a tree that towered above the rest about a hundred yards southwest. If the shooter had Isla there, he'd see Adan coming from every direction. Smart. But Adan hadn't survived two tours in a war zone without knowing what he was getting himself into.

Keeping low, he tracked through a maze of brush and other trees. He'd been right. The Joshua tree ahead had outgrown them all, but from here there was something different. Something…hanging from the tree. The shooter had hung her by her wrists for Adan to see. Nausea churned in his gut. She wasn't moving. Didn't even seem to breathe. Moonlight shifted from behind a cloud overhead, and he realized she'd been stripped down to her slacks and a tank top. He gripped the gun in one hand. Too hard. "Isla."

"You don't have to hide out there in the dirt, Adan Sergeant," an unfamiliar voice said. "Why don't you join us?"

His nerves hit high alert as he considered his next move. The shooter knew his name, was expecting him. If he stood, the bastard could take him out then and there. If he kept his cover, he could be wasting time getting to Isla. Neither option eased the strategic part of his training, but this was Isla. There was nothing strategic or analytical about her. She was all he had left. Adan stood, too exposed for his comfort. Then again, war tended to have that effect on him. Tended to demand this kind of vulnerability from him, but he wouldn't be the one to surrender in the end. "I don't know you."

A dim red light brightened up ahead. A cigarette. Adan could smell it now. Something foreign and familiar.

"You wouldn't." The light was extinguished into the dirt beside a dark outline. "You and I never formally met."

Which meant they'd come across each other by some other means. Adan scanned the length of the shooter armed with his rifle. Less than a hundred yards would be like taking a hammer to an apple for men like them. Too easy. Moonlight glinted off a piece of metal on the man's chest, and recognition flared. "You were in Morocco."

"I was," he said.

"You killed my best friend." The muscles in his jaw ticked under pressure. He'd imagined this day for over a year. Rehearsed conversations. Mapped out exactly what he'd do when he faced the man who'd killed Clint. None of it had played out as he'd expected. Adan's gaze went to Isla still hanging there, unmoving. What had the the gunman done to her?

"It was nothing personal, I assure you." The silhouette stood there like a cardboard cutout. "But considering you're here and Fischer is not, I'm starting to think this might be personal for you. I'll make you a deal. You can have Officer Vachs here. On one condition: you bring me the shipment in the next twenty-four hours."

She was still alive. Adan would agree to anything to save her. "Get out of my way."

"You have twenty-four hours, Sergeant. After that, you'll wish my bullet had finished the job." The shooter's outline disappeared as easily as he'd disappeared from Morocco. Without a trace.

"Isla." Adan had a choice: stop the son of a bitch who'd killed Clint or save Isla. *You gotta protect them. Promise me, Sarge.* He pumped his legs as hard as his body allowed and wrapped both arms around Isla's legs. "Come on, woman. Say something."

He hefted her higher, but the ropes around her wrists caught on the spindles of the Joshua tree. He'd have to cut her down. Scanning the area, he caught sight of a large knife stabbed into the earth. The shooter had left it behind. Adan didn't have time to think about the deal he'd made. There was only Isla. He swiped the blade across the ropes, then dropped it in time to catch her.

Her small frame collapsed over his shoulder. Adan laid her at the base of the tree. Unresponsive. Pressing his ear to her mouth, he heard the slightest exhale. Not watery. Her lungs were fine. It was something else, but the pitch dark only made it that more difficult to get a read on any injuries. "Wake up, Bugs."

Clint's nickname for his wife settled in the air between them. It was a last-ditch effort to get her to come around, but it wasn't working. He ran his hands down her arms, coming into contact with a tourniquet. Blood crusted on the gauze. The bleeding from her bullet wound had slowed. He continued across her shoulders, down her chest and stomach and hips. No wounds. Her legs didn't show any sign of injury, either. He wrapped one cold foot in both hands. The shooter had removed her boots and socks. Experience and inspection of the bottom of her heels supplied the answer he'd been looking for. He tested the muddy dirt beneath where she'd been hung by her wrists.

Not mud. Blood.

It hadn't been enough for the bastard to put a bullet in her side two months ago. The shooter had tried to exsanguinate her. Adan had seen soldiers bled to death in a similar fashion in Middle Eastern prison camps. It had been a message. For him.

Chapter Nine

The lighting in heaven sucked.

Too bright.

Isla turned away from the onslaught, sinking deeper into some kind of scratchy, pillowy cloud. The turn-down service could use some help. She'd have to talk to someone about that.

A consistent beep accentuated the steady painful beat of her heart behind her ears. That was annoying, too. What kind of heaven was this? She peeled her eyelids open. A monitor with green lines and spiky readings crested and troughed a few feet away. She followed a length of clear tubing into the back of her scraped-up hand.

Not heaven.

A hospital.

A groan rumbled through her chest. The same weight she'd experienced while hanging from that tree pressed her deeper into the mattress. If she could call it that. She forced herself to take stock of the room. Simple enough. As long as nothing was broken. She caught sight of the ridiculously handsome and muscled man slouched back in what looked like the most uncomfortable chair on the planet.

He was here. He'd come for her.

She didn't know where that knowledge came from. In fact, she didn't know a whole lot since passing out hanging from a tree and ending up here, but she knew him. He'd gotten her out of there. Just like he'd promised Clint. "I don't suppose you're here to bring me a *viennoiserie*."

Adan startled awake. He unfolded his arm from the other secured in a sling and scanned the room like the good soldier he was supposed to be. Compellingly bright eyes landed on her, and the defensiveness slipped from his expression. The small cuts around his face shifted as he spoke. "Hey. You're awake."

"It appears that way. You look like crap." It wasn't true. If anything he looked…battle-tested. And way more pulled together than she felt at the moment. A tightness charged through her chest as the memories flooded past whatever painkiller they'd given her to lower her defenses. "What happened?"

"You lost a lot of blood. You've had a couple transfusions. Doctors said you'll make a complete recovery as long as you take it easy. The bullet will leave a scar, but I don't have to tell you that." Adan tried to sit straighter in his chair. Bruises shadowed one side of his face in a dark spatter of randomness, and she wanted nothing more than to smooth them away. He'd risked his life for her. Taken a bullet for her. Hunted her down to bring her back. She owed him her life.

"No," she said. "I mean with the case."

"Layton Burgess is dead. Seems whatever he was going to tell us about the group Clint got involved with was enough to kill for," he said.

"They wanted something from me." Isla tried to ignore the warmth in her feet. They'd been wrapped. Because the shooter had cut them open and left her in the middle of the desert. If Adan hadn't been there... "Where's Mazi?"

"The school called Karie Ford when you didn't show to pick her up." His eyes softened the second the subject of her daughter came up. "She's safe, Isla. The ranch is crawling with cops to make sure nobody gets to her."

Isla. Her name sounded...wrong. Maybe she'd imagined it while losing her body's blood supply, but she could've sworn he'd called her by her childhood nickname. The one her grandmother had given her when she'd come home with bugs stuffed in her overalls as a kid. Clint had used it for a while, but he hadn't been out there with her. She'd been out there because of him. "What...what did they tell her?"

"That you got hurt on the job. Your chief made sure not to go into too much detail, but Mazi's worried about you. They all are." His all-too-compelling gaze locked onto her and refused to let up, and a nervousness pricked at the back of her neck. She'd never been nervous around him. Ever. What had changed? "Ford took what happened back to the mayor and lost his voice proving this town needs your department now more than ever. That his investigation will only put doubt in the minds of the townspeople. Not sure how much good it did."

The investigation. She'd forgotten all about that. Easy to do in the midst of dying, she supposed. She forced herself to stare down the length of her body, to prove he didn't have this…hold on her. That what they'd been through hadn't significantly altered their relationship. She swiped at her face with her uninjured arm. Who was she kidding? Her entire body was injured. "And the shooter?"

"Easton Ford tracked him from where I found you, but his trail ended in the mountains. My bet, he had a vehicle waiting or he borrowed Burgess's ATV." Adan's attention battled the uncertainty spreading through her.

It didn't stop everything, though. Images she'd rather forget flickered in her mind. Fischer, the two other men with him, the shooter's face lit by the tip of a cigarette. Pain shot down the length of her body, and she sat a bit straighter. "How…" She tried to clear her throat. "How did we get out of there?"

"Your buddy Kendric," he said. "He finished searching Layton Burgess's house sooner than expected. He tried calling, but when you didn't answer the radio or your phone, he figured he'd check it out. Got to us just in time."

Kendric. She owed him an order from Caffeine and Carbs. "Did he find anything at Burgess's apartment that tells us anything?"

"Yeah." Adan leaned forward in his chair, seemingly realizing he couldn't shift his weight to both elbows. "The place had been ransacked from the look of it before he got there. Took some doing, but he found surveillance photos, entire notebooks filled with notes, shipping manifests, an unhealthy amount of guns and a few other things shoved inside some cut drywall behind the bed. Shooter and his unit must've missed it or been interrupted. From what Kendric and your chief have been able to go through, it looks like Layton Burgess was telling the truth. Clint was involved in the operation with Fischer."

Her stomach clenched as though she'd been physically struck. "Oh."

"Hey." He shoved to his feet, towering over yet never intimidating her. The mattress dipped with his added weight. His ability to read her had always grated on her nerves. Like he could see inside her head. He set one hand over hers against her thigh, and a rush of tears burned in her eyes. "We're going to figure this out. You and I both know Clint wouldn't have gotten involved in something like this unless he had to, and you're safe here. I won't let anyone come for you. All you need to focus on is getting better."

"You mean ignore the fact my husband lied to me? Ignore that he was involved with these people, that he bought a house in the middle of the desert to support their operation, that it got him killed." She shoved her blankets off. Shoved his hand off. She didn't want any of it. The heart rate monitor projected the doubt and anger and humiliation storming inside. "How, Adan? How am I supposed to go home and look at his photos on the wall—photos with Fischer in them—and lie to my daughter about her father being a hero? He wasn't a hero. He was some kind of drug dealer, and now his buddies want to kill me for something I don't have. Tell me how I'm supposed to do this."

Adan's concern stayed in place, but there was a stillness in his jaw with a sharper edge than the rest of his face. "I don't know."

That wasn't the answer she'd expected. She'd wanted him to argue with the evidence. They couldn't prove Clint was involved with the operation. Not without his military records, and every single one of her requests had been shut down. All they had were the words of the men who'd tried to kill them and a paranoid security operator on his way to Dr. Miles's exam room at the funeral home.

"But I know Clint loved you, and he loved Mazi. If he got involved with these people, it had to have been for a reason. He'd never risk your lives unless it was important, and he wouldn't have made me promise to protect you otherwise," he said.

She wanted to believe that. That her husband had pulled her and Mazi into this for a good cause, but if that was the case, why not tell her the truth? Her heart rate normalized the longer Adan kept his gaze settled on her. In a matter of seconds, the echo of PA orders, voices outside the room and the monitors tracking her stats faded. Until there was only Adan. But this time, the shame, the guilt—it stayed put. Isla smoothed the sheets along her waist. "The shooter kept asking me about a shipment of some kind. He said he'd already torn apart my house and was waiting for someone to show at the place in the desert. He thinks I'm hiding it for Clint. That's why they came after us."

"Fischer said the same thing. Right until he lost the ability to speak." Adan maneuvered off the bed and reached for a pitcher of ice water on the table beside the bed. He poured a glass and handed it off to her. Such a simple act, but prominent. Reverberating. "And that you and Mazi would be an example for what happens when one of their people goes rogue."

One of their people. Clint had been one of those people, but her emotional capacity had reached its limit. She couldn't think about what that meant or why her husband of nearly ten years had lied to her in his last days. "Where are they now? The other men who came after us? Fischer and them."

"Fischer disappeared before Easton and Gregson could respond, but he left his friends behind to handle themselves." A wisp of a smile transformed his features into something beautiful and chaotic. Nothing like the composed soldier she'd known going on a decade. "Bills tried to put up a fight. I caught some of it while EMTs were loading you in the ambulance. They never stood a chance against a Green Beret."

"Easton. Should've known." She clutched her glass and took a drink to clear out the last of dirt from her mouth. It should've brought some kind of relief, but knowing the bastards who'd hung her to die were still out there was enough to keep her armed and paranoid. Not the best combination, but it would have to be enough. Otherwise, she and Mazi would never be safe. "Serves them right."

"Isla." Adan's voice dipped as he took his seat at the edge of the mattress again. So close but distanced. Careful. Like he was afraid she'd shatter into a million pieces right there. "Is there anything you can think of—anything about Clint's last days—that would give us an idea of what he took from Fischer's people?"

She studied the water in her glass before taking another drink. The moments before she'd passed out were slightly out of reach, floating there as though she'd gone into that state between wakefulness and sleeping, but there was one thought that stood out among the rest. She'd held out while the shooter had waited for her to die. Thinking back, maybe she'd always suspected Clint had been hiding something. Now…now she knew the truth.

"I don't know what he took. I'm not sure I want to know the details, but…" Isla raised her gaze to Adan's as she tried to let go of the idea her husband had been the hero she'd imagined him to be. "But I think I know where you can find it."

EIGHTEEN HOURS.

That was all he had left to deliver whatever Clint had taken. If he failed, Isla would be the one to pay the price. Her and Mazi. And Adan… He'd be left with nothing all over again.

But he had no intention of handing over anything he recovered.

Adan kicked the solid wood-and-steel plated door with his toe and swung it open. "In you go, kid."

"Why do we have to stay here?" Mazi dragged her bright purple unicorn suitcase behind her. "Why can't I sleep in my bed?"

"I told you, Maz. There's some very bad people looking for us." Isla maneuvered in behind her daughter, her gaze cutting from the too-small kitchen off to the right to the too-small living room on the left. She raised her attention to him as she walked Mazi over the threshold with one useable arm. "Uncle Adan just wants to keep us safe until it all gets worked out. Think of it as that sleepover you wanted."

"I love sleepovers! I'm going to check out my room." Mazi's suitcase fell as the kid ran down the hallway at full steam.

"Down the hall on the right, kid." Adan hefted the unicorn suitcase upright. He'd hauled Isla's overnight bag onto the love seat backed against the living room wall. "I told Officer Majors to help her pack two days of clothes. What the hell did they do? Pack rocks?"

"Probably. Mazi has an entire collection of geodes, and Alma doesn't have the defenses against an eight-year-old." Isla moved deeper into the house, seemingly taking everything in from her position on the brown shag carpeting. "She pretty much gets anything she wants from everyone in the department. Fire and rescue, too. I usually have to be the bad guy and cut them off from spoiling her."

"To be fair, she's worth spoiling." He counted off the rhythm of her breathing as her shoulders rose and fell. Never in his life had he imagined seeing her like this. Bruised, broken, unsure of herself and the lies she'd been told. Alone, even with Mazi in tow. Whenever he'd looked toward the future, Clint had been there.

Adan forced himself to release the handle of her overnight bag, and he stretched his shoulder back to ease some of the tightness. They'd been discharged from the hospital a few hours ago, but going back to their lives—to Isla's house or the station—hadn't been an option. The shooter and Fischer would most likely have eyes on both places. This was the safest bet, but it meant three people in a house sized for two. "Place isn't much, but it'll work. Both bedrooms are at the back, you saw the extent of the kitchen, single bathroom in the hallway. I've got sensors on all the doors and windows. As long as you don't try to open a window or something like that during the night, we should be good."

"This was the safe house you wanted to being me and Mazi to a few days ago?" she asked. "Who lives here?"

"I do." Adan felt too big for the room. Hell, he felt too big for his bones with all the swelling and aches. "It's been empty since I bought it last year. After Clint died. It's titled under one of my government aliases, so you don't have to worry about Fischer finding this place. No one has access to those files."

Truth was, he'd bought this place in case Isla and Mazi had needed him to be close, but that invitation hadn't ever come. It wasn't until she'd been shot two months ago, he found a use for it.

"Okay." She turned to face him. Raising her uninjured arm as though to cross her arms, Isla must've realized she couldn't rely on her defensive habits and lowered her hand back to her side. "I'll go put my stuff in Mazi's room."

"She's only got a twin bed in there," he said.

"That's okay." She reached for her overnight bag.

"I'm used to sleeping with her. She actually has a harder time if she can't see me."

Right. Because of Mazi's nightmares. He'd forgotten about that. Seemed no matter what he did, he was making a mistake. Said the wrong thing. "Then how about I move you both in the main bedroom? It's a bigger bed. More room."

"You're a little bit big for a twin," she said.

"The couch looks…comfortable." It wouldn't be. It was most likely twenty years old, and it was half his size. No. He wasn't looking forward to that, but he'd used rocks for pillows before. He could do it again. All that mattered was Isla and Mazi.

"Adan, stop." She dragged her overnight bag off the couch. It thudded hard against her leg, but Isla wouldn't ever admit if it had hurt. "You've already taken a bullet for me. Almost two. You saved my life out there in the desert, and you look like you're on the verge of collapse. At some point you're going to have to stop sacrificing your needs for us. Let this be a first step. All right? Take the bigger bed."

She didn't wait for him to argue, heading down the hallway toward Mazi's room. Even with the burn of her instructions fresh, a big part of him liked their back-and-forth. Low voices filtered down the hall from the back room. He wasn't alone. For the first time since he'd left the military, he had someone to take care of, to talk to, to laugh with. Hard to do with a bullet wound in his shoulder, but he could do it. And considering Mazi had no filter and insisted on doing everything her way, he was in for a world of the best kind of pain.

All too easily, he could imagine fixing this place up, making it a rightful home and not a last stand. He'd rip out the kitchen, get some kid-safe furniture in here. Mazi could do homework at the kitchen table back by the sliding glass doors leading out to the yard. He'd help her decorate her room any color she wanted for when she came to visit. Isla could sit in a big chair by the oversize stone fireplace with a book while he worked on cooking them something or finished up a project in the garage. After she and Adan had put Mazi to bed, he'd put on a movie for him to ruin with incessant questions and teasing. She might let him hold her hand. Maybe kiss him. He could spend the night showing her exactly how much she'd meant to him all these years.

He could make them happy here.

Adan could see it, so clearly, but the fantasy faded too fast as he remembered the reason Isla and Mazi were here in the first place. That life, the one within reach, wasn't his. It belonged to Clint. Always had, and from the pain-stricken grief he caught on Isla's face when she thought he wasn't looking, it always would be.

Movement registered from the hallway, and Adan forced himself back into the moment. He had a job to do. His personal feelings had no place in this assignment. "You ladies get settled?"

"As much as we could." Isla smiled down at her daughter, stroking Mazi's hair. Before she had a chance to wipe her expression clean, she turned that smile on him.

"Uncle Adan, do you have anything to eat?" Mazi asked.

"Yeah, kid. I asked one of your mom's work buddies to put some stuff in the pantry. Why don't you go see what they brought?" he said.

"Okay!" The eight-year-old tornado practically shook the house as she raced through the kitchen and started going through the cabinets.

"I hope you're ready for the grocery bill that comes with that one. She never stops snacking." Isla's laugh swarmed his head and shot straight to his chest. It was light, and nervous, and held a fraction of the brightness it had once emitted, but he committed it to memory all the same. To have something to hold on to when this case was closed, when he went back to his solitary life, and Isla and Mazi moved on with theirs. Isla hooked her thumb into the back pocket of her jeans. "And thanks for this. Giving us someplace to go and coordinating clean-up efforts with my department. I don't know if I have the stomach to go back to the house just yet."

"Once Kendric is finished processing everything, you can have him bring more of your stuff.

I wasn't sure what you needed." Fantasy was one thing. Knowing what a female partner and her kid needed to get through the day was beyond him. He should've asked Alma to handle Isla's things, too, when he'd run into her at the hospital. "Or if you need me to grab something from the store, monthly products, or anything like that, I can go tonight. Just tell me what you need."

"Did you just offer to buy menstrual products?" she asked.

He didn't understand. "Is that a problem?"

"No. It's sweet, really. Most of the men I've known wouldn't be caught dead in that aisle," she said. "I was just imagining you confused and asking for help trying to decide between light, heavy or overnight tampons."

"Does that mean you need me to go to the store?" he asked.

"You're off the hook, soldier." She patted him on the arm, and a wave of heat seared across his skin, cleansing and pure. It wiped the pain from his muscles and eased the itching beneath his damn sling. It countered the violent and rage-fueled urges he'd been feeding since finding her hanging from that tree. It burned away the loneliness and isolation from the past year. All because of her.

"All I can think about right now is that my house is a crime scene. It took forever for us to find that place," she said. The smile was gone as she watched

Mazi move from one cabinet to the next like a worker bee. "Before he left for his last tour, Clint spent most of his time in the garage at the house we had back east."

Anticipation needled under his skin. "You think he might've hidden what Fischer and the shooter are looking for there?"

"No. I tore that entire house apart after his death looking for anything that might remind me of him." Her voice softened. She dug her uninjured hand into her jeans. "Something I could keep with me. After everything that's happened these past few months, I realize now I was looking in the wrong place. I should've known considering how much money and time he put into it." She tossed him a set of keys. "We need to search his truck."

Chapter Ten

Battle Mountain's impound lot consisted of six parking stalls, a rolling chain-link gate with a padlock and a single guard at the entrance in a tiny booth behind the station. Tonight, it seemed Macie Barclay had drawn the short straw. "Don't you look nice with your tight ponytail not pulling the joy out of your face. Almost didn't recognize you with your hair down, Vachs. Thought I might have to pull out Bettie June."

"I'm not on duty." Isla couldn't help but smile at the Ruger snub nose revolver Macie had introduced to the entire department and over the radio on account of killers running rampant in town. The dispatcher hadn't been wrong about that this week. "How's it going here?"

"Boring. The voices in my head started fighting, and at least one of my personalities ran off." Macie's eyes brightened, and Isla knew the moment she'd set sights on the mountain of attitude behind her. "But tonight just happens to be looking up."

"Ms. Barclay." Adan nodded in such a gentle-manly fashion, Isla thought he might've reenlisted.

"Mr. Sergeant, I was hoping you hadn't left town yet." Despite her sarcastic nature and individual taste for living in tree houses and pissing off Easton Ford every chance she got, Macie Barclay had become the cornerstone of the entire Battle Mountain Po-lice Department. She was meticulously organized, intelligent beyond the dolled-out facade she exhib-ited for the public, and had a way of convincing just about anyone to see things her way. Especially men.

"All right. Enough of that." Isla knocked on the booth, and Macie's dreamlike expression evapo-rated, almost as short-lived as her transformation to a blonde had been that one time, when she'd dyed her fire-engine red hair. "As much as I'd love to catch up since yesterday, we're not here for a social visit or for you to read our tarot cards. Although that last one was surprisingly accurate, we need to get into my truck."

"You don't have to be crazy to hang out with me for more than few minutes, you know. I'll train you, Vachs." Macie drew back into the booth and hit the button to engage the gate. "Wouldn't take long, either. You seem like a fast learner."

"I'll keep that in mind." Isla moved to wait for the gate to open wide enough for her and Adan to slide through and waved. "Thanks, Macie."

They hadn't made it more than a few steps before

he asked the one thing she was hoping wouldn't come up during this search. "You let Macie read your tarot cards?"

"Every once in a while." The single motion-censored light in the lot came to life and reflected off the deep red paint of Clint's truck. It looked the same as it always did. Only she knew as they got closer that she'd be able to pick out the bullet hole in the engine block. Considering how proud Clint had been of the monster and how many hours he'd put into it, she'd expected it to be bulletproof. Then again, it hadn't really been about the truck, had it? Everything that had happened these past couple of months—the shootings, her abduction, Layton Burgess's death— had all come to pass because of what Clint could've hidden inside it. "In my line of work and as a single mom, it helps to have a heads-up, don't you think?"

"What did you last reading say?" he asked. "The one you said was so accurate."

His arm brushed against her as they reached the passenger-side door of the truck. They must've looked pathetic right then under the motion light. Both of them wrapped in slings, peppered in bruises and barely able to stay upright, but it all seemed kind of fitting, too. Nothing about her and Adan's relationship had come easy. The first time Clint had brought him home, she'd accidentally broken his nose tossing a frozen can of orange concentrate during breakfast. They'd both come back from their one and only camping trip with pneumonia from working on the fire all night. And Clint's death…had broken them both. Her husband had been their rock, their support, and then he hadn't been there at all. What they had now had been forged in the heat of a battle she never wanted to face, but of all the partners to get her and Mazi through it, she trusted Adan. He would keep his word.

"Two months ago, before the first shooting, she told me pain was coming, more than I think I can handle, but that I would get through it." Now that Isla thought about it, Macie might be a witch. How else would she have known about the plague of crime and murder that had descended on Battle Mountain?

"That's pretty heavy stuff." Adan wrenched the truck door open and unpocketed one of the flashlights they'd brought along. "You believe her?"

"Kind of hard not to when you think about why we're in the middle of a parking lot searching my truck." She froze. She'd never laid claim to this monstrosity. It had always been Clint's truck. Clint's project. Clint's pride and joy. Isla opened the back passenger door and tossed the floor mats. Embarrassment shot through her at all the gum wrappers, remnants of cheesy fish crackers and wood chips from the park in every nook and cranny of the back seat. Apparently, they should've brought a vacuum. She brushed as much as she could onto the pavement. Nervous energy simmered under her skin. "She told me the only way I'd get through it was with help from an old friend."

Adan swung the flashlight into the back seat. "I'm not that old."

Her laugh eased past her lips, but something along with it, too. Release. With him, it was easy to imagine grief didn't have a hold on her, despite the constant reminder of why Adan had come into her life in the first place. The heaviness that had consumed her life didn't seem so weighty right then. It felt like she was finally able to breathe. Because of him. "Didn't anyone ever tell you denial is the first stage of acceptance?"

"Keep talking that way, and you can fend for yourself for dinner," he said.

"Wouldn't want that." A genuine smile tugged at one corner of her mouth. Foreign and unexpected. This. This was what she'd missed the most after Clint had died. The jokes, the banter, the comfort of having someone to talk to, even if it was just about a tarot card reading. The chief, Macie, Easton, Karie— they'd all been there for her when she'd come to Battle Mountain and after she'd gotten shot. They were her friends, sure, but Adan... He was so much more.

He was a lifeline in the middle of the hurricane determined to drag her under the surface. Her one escape. When he looked at her, she felt it. She felt heard and cared for and important. Her grief hadn't just been about losing her husband or her fear for Mazi's future. She'd lost a piece of herself, but worse, she'd lost someone to love her. After everything Adan had done, for her, for Mazi, it was easy to imagine he shared some kind of attachment to them. Because as it turned out, she was getting a little attached to him.

Adan pulled a blade from his waistband and held it up in the yellow overhead light. "Are you ready for this?"

He didn't have to elaborate. They'd come here to search the truck, and they weren't leaving this lot until they had what the shooter had killed so many people for. Isla nodded and backed out of the truck.

The sound of tearing fabric reached her ears. She'd expected this to be harder. For her to feel gutted with every stroke of the blade, but the regret, the guilt, the shame—it never came. Stuffing fell around Adan's boots as he moved from the front passenger seat to the back. Still, the crushing weight of emotion never washed in to drown her. "Found something."

He backed out of the truck as she moved in. Holstering his blade, he dragged a duffel bag from beneath one of the back seats. Where Mazi usually sat. The bag was identical to the one they'd found in the desert

All this time, Clint had hidden, under his child's seat, something that could get his family killed. "I didn't know those seats could be moved."

Adan dropped the duffel at their feet. "From the look of the weld marks and stitching, I'd say it was a custom job. Probably something he did himself considering he hadn't wanted to bring anyone else into this. You want to do the honors?"

Her mouth dried. What was she going to find in there? Another change of clothes, some food in case Clint had to go on the run? Drugs? She had the right to know about it all. Crouching, Isla slipped a glove onto her uninjured hand. Her balance wavered as she reached for the bag, but Adan was there, holding her up with the strength of his leg at her back. And wasn't that the ultimate metaphor? Clint was dead because of his lies, and Adan had her back. She unzipped the bag and spread the mouth wider.

"I don't get it." She raised her gaze to Adan standing over her. "This is what Fischer and the shooter are willing to kill for? A bag of cash?"

It didn't make sense. Of all the things the men who'd tried to kill her could've been after, cash was the most easily replaceable. She'd at least expected drugs as Layton Burgess had theorized, even artifacts considering Clint and his unit had been stationed in the Middle East. Not this.

Concentration etched deep in Adan's expression. He crouched beside her, reaching in with his own gloved hand. He picked up a single hundred-dollar bill. Discarding that one, he picked up another, then rummaged through the whole bag. Upwards of over a hundred thousand dollars, if he had to guess. "They're counterfeit."

"How can you tell?" The only way she'd been able to identify a fake bill was with the marker stuffed in her desk at the station. And she hadn't even used it. She wasn't sure any of the officers in the department had. Isla picked up one of the bills. It looked pretty real to her.

"The ink ran on this one." Adan handed off the bill in his hand.

He was right. She could still see the light imprint of a one where the ink had smeared. "Okay. So this used to be a one-dollar bill, and Fischer and his men are printing over them with hundred-dollar stamps."

That was what this was all about? Printing fake money? And it had been in her truck all this time, beneath her daughter's seat. Her heart broke a little more as the truth pierced through her determination to keep her husband atop the pedestal she'd put him on years ago. She tossed the bill back into the duffel bag. "Clint was involved in a counterfeit scheme."

He still didn't believe it. Even a couple hours later.

But the proof was right there on the desk.

"It all comes down to counterfeit cash, then." Chief Ford angled behind his desk. The bag they'd recovered from Isla's truck sat open in front of him. "They're not perfect, but I can see the draw. Print your own cash, buy up whatever you want. Do we know who this shipment was meant for?"

Adan pressed his back into the glass window overlooking the rest of the station. Macie Barclay had taken up her position at the front desk while Officers Majors and Gregson chatted in the break room. Gregson kissed his partner before donning his jacket and heading for the front of the station, and Adan's gut clenched.

Outside looking in, that was a real partnership, the kind where two people had each other's back in the field and at home. Seemed everyone in this station had found their other half. The chief and the coroner, Easton and his district attorney, Majors and Gregson. Even Kendric Hudson had an FBI investigator and a toddler on the hook. Isla deserved a partner like that, someone to have her back, to take the burden off from raising a wild child on her own, to be loved.

He could be her partner. If she'd let him.

"The shooter said he had powerful employers, that we didn't want to make them mad." Isla leaned forward in her seat, settling her uninjured arm on her knee. The bruises around her eye had gone from dark purple and blue to yellow around the edges. She was on the mend and still just as beautiful. He just had to keep her alive long enough to get to the finish line. "My guess, these guys got mixed up with organized crime or a cartel. They produce the cash in exchange for the real deal. Question is, where are they getting it from?"

"Iraq." The pieces were starting to fall into place. Adan forced himself to focus on the moment. Not on what he would never have. "The government sent millions of cold hard cash into the Middle East during the war. Mostly one-dollar bills packed into shipping containers. It was supposed to fund operations in an effort to put us ahead of the game. No red tape. Our unit came across a container during a routine training exercise outside of Kabul. Must've been at least a million inside. We reported it up the chain. Were told to walk away." Adan gripped the back of one of the leather chairs across from the chief's desk. "Obviously Fischer and the guys he works with had other ideas."

"It makes sense. The treasury goes to extreme lengths to guard the recipe for the paper used for bills. They have a bunch of screening tests they use to identify counterfeit cash. Taking a low denomination bill and repurposing it cuts out a lot of problems." Isla shoved to her feet and bit down on her thumbnail, an old habit she'd picked up after having Mazi. It was her concentration face. "That still leaves a matter of washing the one-dollar bills and printing the hundred-dollar emblem onto the paper. Not to mention getting it into the States without raising suspicion."

"One problem at a time," Ford said.

At least now they knew why Clint had been killed. They had answers, even if they didn't like them. "Clint took a shipment obviously meant for Fischer's high-powered friends and hid it for over a year. He's scared, desperate. This bag was most likely the first delivery, proof of what Fischer could get his hands on. Without it, they have nothing," Adan said. "That's why the shooter is the one calling the shots. He's not military. At least not ours. My bet, he was sent by whoever wants their hands on this shipment."

"So we use it to draw them out and end this." Isla's gaze locked on his, and the pain in his shoulder, the exhaustion pulling his body apart, the past, the future—everything dissipated. In that moment, it was just the two of them.

"Then we'll need to do it fast." The chief maneuvered around his desk. "I can get in touch with the DEA, try to get a list of organizations specializing in fake cash, but now that we've got two bodies, the mayor isn't happy." Ford settled back on the edge of his desk, arms folded over his chest. "He's talking about starting over with a clean slate."

"What does that mean?" Isla straightened a bit more.

"He's bringing in another department to run the investigation into your shooting and the deaths of Gail Oines and Layton Burgess," Ford said. "When he does, neither you nor Mr. Sergeant here will be allowed anywhere near this case. And neither will I."

"He can't do that." Her voice notched a bit higher. "The only reason we've gotten this far is because of what Adan and I have uncovered. They can't just shut us out."

Adan read between the lines. She didn't want to be shut out, and considering the connection between Clint, her shooting outside the fire station and Mazi's future, he didn't blame her.

"He's the mayor, Isla. He runs this town, and from the townspeople's point of view, Battle Mountain PD isn't doing enough to keep them safe." Ford hoisted his shoulders higher. "He can't ignore them."

"He doesn't care about the people here. He just wants to be reelected next year," Isla said.

"Either way, he has the final say." Acceptance bled into the chief's eyes. "As soon as the investigators from Montrose are here, we're out. All of us."

"Not if I have anything to say about it." Isla wrenched open the door leading out into the smallest bullpen Adan had ever seen. Two desks, both of which seemed to be used by more than one officer each. She headed for the front door and shoved through the glass.

"I take it she just heard about the mayor's plan." Macie Barclay smoothed her hair as she peeled her headset free. "That needle-nose penguin doesn't know what's good for this town. Just what's good for his ego."

"Guess that means you're on the outs, too," he said.

"Me? Oh, I'm not going anywhere." Macie shook her head. "None of those shiny new investigators are going to want to answer the phone. They'll be focused on finding that shooter of yours and taking credit for closing two of our murder cases. They won't give me the time of day, which is good because then they won't know what hit them."

His brows drew inward. "You're going to sabotage their investigation."

"Maybe a little." She pinched her thumb and index finger together. "Just long enough to give you and Vachs a head start. I can't say it will work or that the chief won't find out what I'm doing, but I know what your partner has been through. She's earned to be the one to solve this thing. Not some cleanup crew who doesn't give a damn about this town."

He'd underestimated Macie Barclay.

"Thanks, Macie." He meant it. Because the dispatcher was right. Isla needed to be the one to see this through. She needed the closure, and to know she and Mazi would be safe once the shooter was behind bars.

"You're welcome." She held out her hand in expectation. "Now all I will require is a vial of your blood as payment."

"Pretty sure losing more blood will kill me, but I'll see what I can do." Adan followed after Isla, finding her in front of the station.

She'd lost the tightness in her shoulders and neck, hugging her injured arm close. Short hair brushed into her face as she stared down the length of Main Street. "This place used to be safe. Tourists would come here to vacation at the lake or hike the trails. The mining companies stocked our stores and kept us employed before the money dried up. Now look at us. We've got serial killers, bombers, a freaking sniper." She shook her head. "These people are scared it's never going to end. So am I. I signed on as a reserve officer to protect my daughter. Turns out her own father is the one who put her in danger. Pretty soon, I won't even be able to find out why."

He didn't know how to argue with that. This whole thing—all the evidence—pointed to Clint as an operator in Fischer and the shooter's organization. The go bag at the house in the desert, the counterfeit cash hidden in the truck—there had to be something they were missing. Had to be a reason Clint had gone rogue. "You're a good mom, Isla. You were a good wife. I don't know why this is happening or how Clint's involved, but there's not a single bone in your body that believes this is over. We're going to figure this out. Together. I give you my word."

Her mouth quirked. "You remind me of him sometimes. They say you're a combination of the five people you spend the most time with, and I see Clint in you. Your confidence, for one. He never met a challenge he wasn't willing to face head-on. Didn't like anyone else making decisions for him, either, but none of that was why I fell in love with him." Her eyes glittered with unshed tears. The past few days had taken a toll, and her guard had started to break under the pressure. "He was loyal. To me, his family, his country and his friends. Long before he joined the military. I think he got that from you."

She crossed the sidewalk toward the patrol car parked a few spots down.

Pure need had him reaching out. He secured his hand around her uninjured arm and dragged her back into his orbit. Right where he needed her. Her mouth parted as he stared down at her, her attention dipping to his mouth. "Can I kiss you?"

One second. Two.

Her throat constricted on a deep swallow, and she raised her gaze back to him. "Yes."

Adan pressed his mouth to hers, and a whole world of color he hadn't known existed materialized around him. His senses rocketed into overdrive until all he felt was Isla. Lean muscle, soft skin, full lips. She tasted of mint gum and wildfire, and he couldn't get enough.

A laugh trilled through the night as another couple walked by, and Adan backed off. The middle of Main Street probably wasn't the best place to lay one on her, but he hadn't been able to wait. Heat slid up his neck and into his face. He wasn't one for embarrassment, and he sure as hell didn't regret that kiss, but right then, he was in unknown territory.

Isla fisted his T-shirt and pulled him toward the patrol car. "Come on, Sergeant. Let's get you home."

Chapter Eleven

It didn't matter how many sticks of gum she'd chewed or how many times she'd brushed her teeth. She could still taste him. A mix of something dark and invigorating but fresh at the same time.

When Adan had kissed her, she hadn't been Isla Vachs, Clint Vach's wife. She'd just been herself. A woman who'd lost her husband, who was more than a single mom, who missed physical connection and someone a little more mature than an eight-year-old to talk to at night. Someone who desired and wanted to be desired.

Adan made her feel it all.

He'd laid claim to her in a single kiss right there in the middle of the street. Now, as she studied her reflection in the dusty mirror and combed her wet hair, all she could think about was what had changed between them. How she'd gone from blaming him for Clint's death to wanting…more. Not just physically. Emotionally. Mentally.

Her hair caught in her wedding band as she ran

through it one more time. She set down the comb on the small vanity, letting the overhead light catch the diamonds. They still glittered, though not as brightly as they used to, and she couldn't help but see herself in that comparison. She'd been hanging on to Clint for ten years. Even after his death, she just couldn't seem to let go. While he'd loved her for her independent attributes and passions when they'd met, he'd been the star of their marriage and Mazi's whole world. He'd been the one their friends wanted to invite over for Super Bowl parties, who went out of his way to ensure his unit kept in touch and helped others prepare for tour. She'd followed him through his career, like a secondary character in his story, and it hadn't even been that hard. Because she'd loved him. In the end…she'd just been a planet in his orbit. Substantial but muted. Like the diamonds.

But Adan had made her feel like she'd caught fire. One kiss. That was all it had taken for her to not recognize the woman in the mirror. He'd stripped her free of her past and given her something she'd never thought possible. Hope for the future.

Isla pulled her wedding band free, careful not to hinge her arm too much. Her skin had pitted and curved around the metal as she'd gained and lost weight through pregnancy and postpartum recovery, like it had become part of her. In reality, it had. Clint had, but he wasn't here anymore.

And she couldn't hang on to a ghost anymore.

She slipped the band into her sweats and left the

bathroom. Every step shot pain through the bottoms of her feet. Thankfully, the shooter hadn't cut too deep, but he'd gotten his message across loud and clear. He'd marked her for the rest of her life. Anytime she took a step, she'd feel his influence in her life. Even if the cuts healed and scarred over.

Low laughs and teasing emanated from the kitchen, and she found both Adan and Mazi at the kitchen table covered from waist to head in chocolate syrup with innocent looks on their faces.

"She started it." Adan pointed at Mazi with the end of his spoon.

"Did not!" Mazi catapulted a spoonful of vanilla ice cream across the table. Adan dodged at the last second, and the ice cream slid down the sliding glass doors behind them. "You threw a piece of banana at me. I couldn't let your insubordination stand."

"Wow." Her inner control freak, the part of her that wanted all the pieces of her life to fit perfectly, demanded she start cleaning. But over the course of the past few days, Isla had gotten tired. Of the pain in her arm, of the pulsing headache at the back of her skull, of her grief, of her need to have everything in place in her life. She'd spent the past year still living for someone who was dead. All in an attempt to keep being the wife Clint had deserved. She took in the discarded banana peels, a line of caramel across the table and the smile etched on Mazi's face. "Did you at least save any for me?"

That smile widened impossibly further.

"Pull up a chair." Adan shoved to his feet and rounded the table back into the kitchen behind her. "What kind of toppings do you like? We've got chocolate chips, syrups, caramel, strawberries, hot fudge. You name it."

"I didn't think ice cream sundaes were part of safe house living. I've been in the wrong line of work." She sat by Mazi and rubbed her daughter's back. Half turning in her chair, she watched Adan cross from one side of the kitchen to the other trying to gather up anything she might want. It was sweet, the way he'd full-on committed to taking care of them. Then again, that was Adan. Always had been, and warmth flooded her chest. She hadn't ever expected her and Mazi to end up like this—without Clint or as targets—but of all the people she trusted to protect them, to care about them, it was Adan she could rely on, through and through. He was everything she needed right now. "Do you have any sprinkles?"

That half smile of his hiked at one corner of his mouth. "Yeah, I got sprinkles."

Her heart hiccupped, and in that moment she saw what Macie Barclay had seen. A hardworking mountain of muscle and danger any woman with a pulse would want in her life. The minute she'd met him she knew Adan Sergeant would go down with the ship to keep any relationship he had alive, and he hadn't disappointed her in the least. This place... This safe house? Her gut said he'd bought it to be in Battle Mountain. To be here for her and Mazi if and when they needed him, and she needed him. Not just for this investigation or to keep saving her life. For so much more.

Adan returned with an oversize bowl filled to the brim with vanilla ice cream, hot fudge and a pile of Christmas sprinkles.

"Mommy, your ring is gone." Mazi shoveled another spoonful into her mouth, saving the walls and Adan's shirt. "Did you lose it?"

Tightness closed in around her throat as Adan's gaze dropped to her hand for the briefest of moments, but she wouldn't lie to her daughter. "No, baby. I took it off. See?" Isla unpocketed her ring and handed it off to Mazi. "When you're big enough and you find someone you want to marry, maybe you'll be the one to keep wearing it."

"Cool!" Mazi tipped the band this way and that to make the diamonds sparkle, but it was the weight of Adan's attention that pulled Isla's gaze up. "I'm going to go put it on my necklace."

Mazi darted off down the hall, always on the move. And now loaded with sugar before bed.

She couldn't bring herself to look at Adan's face, but she'd bet her measly paycheck he'd read everything in hers. Circling her spoon around in her melting ice cream, she sat there more exposed than she'd ever felt before. She'd taken her wedding ring off. Kind of hard to ignore. Her stomach flipped the longer he studied her. "You can stop staring at me and just ask me what you want to ask."

"Is it safe to give Mazi a sleeping pill?" He set his uninjured elbow on the table, barely missing a line of caramel. "Because I have the feeling us getting her to bed will be impossible."

She couldn't help but laugh. The nervousness that had burned through the last of her energy reserves vanished. How did he do that? How did he make her feel so…accepted? So worthy and deserving? Isla collected Mazi's mess and took it to the kitchen sink. "Us? No, no, no. You gave her the ice cream. You're the one who gets to put her to bed."

"Is that a no on the sleeping pill?" Adan cleared off the rest of the table and followed her into the kitchen. The space shrunk the second he stepped beside her, and her core temperature notched a few more degrees.

"Good luck in there, soldier." She slapped him on the shoulder. "You're going to need it."

He didn't need it. Because within minutes of getting to her room, Mazi had passed out on the bed, Isla's wedding ring in her small hand. She watched from the doorframe as Adan set the band on the nightstand and tucked Mazi fully into bed. Only thousands of hours of military training could get that girl under the covers for the night. He caught her watching him in his peripheral vision just before clicking off the light on the bedside table, and Isla backed out of the room.

Adan closed Mazi's door behind him. "Mission accomplished."

"Don't pretend you did any work." Isla tried to keep her voice down. "She was exhausted the minute we picked her up from the ranch. Half the work was done for you."

Adan leaned into the wall in front of her, those compelling hazel eyes seemingly memorizing everything he could about her. Like she was the only thing worth looking at. It was a very dangerous thing to be the center of this man's world but thrilling at the same time. "You're jealous. I bet I beat some kind of record, and you're just a sore loser."

"Maybe." She set her head against the wall. "What now?"

Adan reached for her left hand, smoothing his thumb over the divot where her ring used to be. Warmth and a little bit of nervousness washed through her. He'd never touched her like this. Not before he'd kissed her anyway. Any time they'd been close to one another, she'd tried to avoid skin-to-skin contact, and a part of her had forgotten what it felt like. "Now I tuck you into bed."

Emotion surged through her chest. "You don't have to do that, Adan. I'm perfectly capable of taking care of myself. I've been doing it for years. I even take care of an eight-year-old pretty well."

"I know." He slid closer, keeping hold of her hand. He maneuvered around her without letting go, and pulled her down the short hallway to the other bedroom. He held her up when all she wanted to do was collapse from the weight of the past few days. Not to mention the constant energy it took for her body to heal from two bullet wounds. "Which is why it's time for you to let someone else take over."

"I'm not sure I know how to do that." Goose bumps trailed up her arm as he settled her on the edge of the bed. "How to let go."

Adan closed the bedroom door behind them and turned back to face her. "That's what I'm here for."

THE CLATTER OF plates had him reaching for the gun in his nightstand.

Adan stripped back the bedding and got to his feet. Another scrape of ceramic. It took a couple seconds to confirm the security system was still active from the panel he'd installed in the bedroom, and the tension drained. He studied the empty bed and scrubbed a hand down his face to ease the surging panic. Not an intruder.

He replaced the gun in the nightstand and closed the drawer. Hell, he'd woken up alone for the past year. It would take a couple more days to get used to having someone else in the house. And this early.

He took care of his morning business and switched out the gauze over the bullet wound in his shoulder. The attending at the hospital had been able to remove the bullet easily enough, but Adan had made a mess of his shoulder. He had a bit more movement today, and the swelling had at least gone down some, but it would take another six to eight weeks for the skin to stitch itself back together and few months of physical therapy to get back to where he'd started. Dressing, he worked his arm into the sling. Ready for anything waiting on the other side of the door.

Adan reached for the doorknob.

The door jerked open and slammed into his chest. The force nearly knocked him backward.

"Uncle Adan, we made breakfast!" Mazi's announcement was partnered with a toss of sparkly confetti before the eight-year-old disappeared back down the hallway.

He spat a piece out that had caught on his lip. What the hell had just happened?

He followed a glittery trail of pink, purple and silver stars into the front room. Mazi twirled in a sweatshirt and jeans that looked too short for her, her hair perfectly styled with waves like her mom's. In the middle of a glitter disaster. "I'm dreaming, aren't I? This is a nightmare I'm going to wake up from any moment, and there will not be glitter stuck in my couch or carpet—" A chunk of confetti fell from his head. "Or my hair."

"I was hoping she'd let you sleep in." Isla penetrated his peripheral vision, offering a steaming cup of coffee. Her arm brushed against his and triggered a whole new round of heat they hadn't been able to douse the night before. "Drink up. It's Saturday, and Karie Ford can't watch Mazi today. This is just the beginning."

"Are you always up this early?" His brain was still

trying to catch up with the impromptu dance party happening in the middle of his living room.

"Why do you think I'm so cranky all the time?" She took a sip from her mug, accentuating full lips he'd had the pleasure of tasting all over again last night. Right until they'd realized they were too tired for anything else and fell into an exhausted sleep curled up next to each other. "You've lived through shelling and explosions during your tours, right?"

"Yeah. Why?" he asked.

"This is worse." A hint of her brilliant smile killed the second-guessing and doubt about his decision creeping in from the back of his mind. "This comes with glitter and unicorns." She laughed as his mouth fell open. "Come on. I made breakfast."

He followed the lingering scent of bacon and eggs to a table full of fruits, chocolate chip muffins and a crispy-looking serving of hash browns. Adan didn't know where to start. No one had made him a meal like this. "You did all this?"

"Mazi helped." She pulled out the chair where he'd sat last night during his and Mazi's food fight and took a seat. Not a single glob of ice cream on the walls, floors or the table. Like it had never happened. Isla served herself some eggs, strawberries and a muffin. "She wanted to thank you for letting us stay here. I'm not sure if you can tell, but she's having a blast."

"I think I can taste her excitement in the piece of confetti I swallowed." He took his seat at the head of table, next to her. "This is…amazing. You didn't have to go through all this trouble. I think there are some granola bars in the pantry."

"It wasn't any trouble. Mazi and I love cooking together on Saturday mornings. It's kind of our ritual since Clint died. It's the only time school and work don't get in the way. We just get to hang out together, the two of us." She poured herself a glass of juice. "Besides, you went out of your way to bring us here, and I wanted to thank you. For everything, especially last night."

He wasn't a man to turn down a great meal, or a woman who so obviously had just needed someone to take the weight of the world off her shoulders. Only it wasn't just any woman. It was Isla. "You're welcome, but if I'm being honest, I've been looking forward to last night for a long time."

A beautiful shade of pink flared up her neck and into her face. Isla cast a glance toward Mazi in the living room. "It was…nice. I, uh—" she cleared her throat and slid her uninjured hand up his arm "—was thinking we might continue our conversation later today."

"Is that so?" Adan leveraged his forearm across the table and leaned into her. "I suppose that's something that can be arranged once that one wears herself out."

A full-fledged smile broke across Isla's face, and she closed the distance between them. She set her mouth against his and kissed him with a slowness that drove him wild. "You have no idea what you've gotten yourself into, do you?"

"Should I be scared?" He secured her hand in his, kissing the scrapes and bruises along her knuckles.

"You might skate by without any permanent damage." Isla's gaze cut to the living room, and she pulled away to sit back in her seat as Mazi charged into the kitchen. "Maz, you've had your fun with the confetti. See if you can find the vacuum and start cleaning it up, please. I'm sure Adan doesn't want to find it stuck to his clothes after you and I go back home."

Home. Damn, the world just refused to slow down. He'd given some thought about what would happen once this investigation was over, but the idea of Isla and Mazi leaving didn't sit right. He'd taken his discharge from the army and gone straight into protecting Mazi and Isla when he'd gotten stateside. Everything he'd done for the past year had been for them. Coming to Battle Mountain, buying this place, spending his days surveilling and researching. His skin burned where she'd touched him, like before. Only this time Adan had the distinct feeling it wouldn't fade with time. She'd branded him, inside and out.

"I don't want to go back home." Mazi grabbed a strawberry from the center of the table. "This place is awesome, and my room is so much bigger here. It's closer to school and my friends. Not out in the middle of nowhere."

A weak smile played across Isla's mouth. She gifted

Adan an apologetic glance before focusing on Mazi. "Honey, I told you. We're only here for a couple days. Just until I close this case. After that, we're going to go back home. Our house. Where all our stuff is."

"No!" Mazi's face crumpled in a whirlwind of tears Adan hadn't expected. "All that's there is Dad's stuff, but he's not. I don't want to go back. I want to stay here with Uncle Adan so I don't have to be sad ever again." The eight-year-old raced down the hallway and punctuated her upset with slamming the bedroom door.

"I'm so sorry. I'm sure fighting is the last thing you need from us while we're here. I just haven't really told her anything since the shooting three nights ago, and she's confused and scared." Isla got to her feet and smoothed invisible lines from the front of her T-shirt. "Keep eating. I'll go talk to her."

"Isla." He wrapped one hand around her wrist as she maneuvered past him. He didn't know anything about eight-year-old girls. He wasn't a parent, and he sure as hell hadn't been prepared for a face full of glitter first thing this morning. This was Isla's world. This had been Clint's world, and he'd been the outsider looking in, wishing he'd had it all. But his best friend was gone, and the man's little girl needed to know she was still the center of someone's universe. "Let me talk to her."

Surprise flittered across Isla's face. Her mouth parted as though she was ready to argue. "Okay."

Adan retraced his earlier path, following the mess

of confetti and stars right to Mazi's temporary bedroom. He knocked softly. "Mazi, can I come in?"

"Go away." Something hit the door, and the entire thing shook. From the impact, he bet a pillow.

"I just want to talk to you for a second," he said.

Quiet sobs reached through the door, and his heart threatened to break in two. He could just imagine how easy it would be to kill anyone who made Mazi cry like this in the future. "Fine."

He swung the door inward and caught sight of her on the floor against the opposite side of the bed. "Hey, kid."

"I already know what you're going to say." She brushed one hand down her face and clenched something in the other.

"That would be some kind of magic trick. I don't even know what I'm going to say." Adan rounded the end of the bed and took a seat beside her against the frame. Hell, she must've tried to pack her whole room in that suitcase. She'd claimed nearly every inch he'd had to spare. "I just wanted to make sure you were okay."

"I like it here. I don't want to go home." She refused to look at him.

He nodded, his knees hiked close to his chest. How she sat like this was beyond him, but Mazi also didn't have over two hundred pounds to haul around. The object she held on to slipped from her hand, and a single silver dog tag slid to the end of the chain. Clint's. And right beside it, Isla's wedding band. Air pressurized in his chest. "Have I ever told you about how your dad and I became friends?"

Watery eyes settled on him, and she shook her head.

"Your dad saved me from the worst beating of my life," he said. "He stepped in while everyone else at school watched. He fought for me, and when it was over, he dragged me back to his house. I was scared, like you're scared now. I didn't want to go back to school because there was a good chance it would just happen again, but your dad said something I'll never forget."

"What did he say?" Mazi asked.

Emotion charged up his throat as he compared the boy he'd known to the man who'd been shot down last year. "He told me being scared doesn't stop bad things from happening in your life. It just makes you stop trying to live the life you've been given."

Chapter Twelve

Those words played on a loop through her mind.

Clint had said that exact phrase when he'd asked her to marry him all those years ago, when he'd promised he would be there for her, love her, and told her he wanted her with every fiber of his being. And she'd said yes. Months later, she'd given her own vow to do the same.

And at the slightest hint of doubt, she'd thrown it all away.

Isla pulled away from Mazi's door, which was cracked open, and headed straight toward the bedroom where she'd spent the night kissing another man. A man very much not her husband. A man who'd somehow convinced her to forget she'd lived an entire life before that first bullet had gone through her side.

Her inhale resonated in her chest. She shook her hands out as the guilt and grief clawed through her chest, aggravating the wound in her arm. Damn this sling. Damn the pain in her side. Damn the bruises across her chest. She ripped it over her head. A different kind of pain had taken hold. Too familiar, too easy to feed.

Clint was dead. He'd lied to her about the house in the desert and his bag of fake cash stashed in his truck, but he'd still been her husband. He'd still fought for his country and loved his daughter and had taken care of his family. He was still part of her.

"Hey. Well, it went better than I thought it would. She'll be okay. She's stronger than she lets on." Adan came into room behind her, one hand smoothing down her arm. "She's been through a lot this past year with Clint gone. You both have. She might just need some time to work through it all."

Isla couldn't answer, could barely manage to catch her breath. She stepped out of his hold. "Please don't touch me."

"Everything okay?" He didn't try to come near her as she retreated to the far side of the room.

"Uh, no." She swiped her palm across her forehead. She could feel her heartbeat in her wound. It was out of control. She wouldn't be surprised if she started bleeding again. "Not really."

"What's going on?" he asked.

"This… Being here. Being with you." She could barely get the words out as what was left of her world crashed down around her. "The ice cream parties and breakfasts, the kissing and the talk you had with Mazi. It's… It's all just a bit much."

Adan didn't answer right away. He just looked

at her as though he could already see the final outcome of this conversation. In an instant, he seemed
so much…bigger. Like he'd been trying to fit into
her world rather being himself and suddenly had
been set free.

"I thought I could do it. I thought I could move
on, but what you said to Mazi a few minutes ago…"
Thoughts lined up from a tornado of chaos into three
words. She locked her gaze on him, and the storm
receded as quickly as it had knocked her off-balance.
"You're not him. You're not my husband. You're not
Mazi's father."

He straightened into his classic guarded position,
shoulders back, chin parallel to the floor. Like he was
back in the military, on alert. "I know that."

"Do you? You certainly tried to step into his shoes
without hesitation these past few days, and I was convinced. To the point I didn't even notice how easily
you'd slid into our lives." She was finally able to take
a full breath. Her hand felt so naked without her wedding ring. She needed it back. "I know Clint made
you promise to look out for us, but I don't think he'd
want…this." She motioned between them.

"What do you want, Isla?" Adan took a step forward but stopped as she countered. He pointed to the
floor. "Forget about Clint, forget about what's best
for Mazi or what you think my game is here. What
do you want right now?"

Nobody had ever asked her that. Everything she'd
done—everything she was—had been to live up to

someone else's needs and expectations. As a military wife, as a mother and then a single mother, as an EMT and a reserve officer. She'd been playing by everyone else's rules without consideration for her own wants. Tears burned in her eyes as she thought about his question. She hugged her arm into her chest. "I want to go back. To the way things were."

Disappointment flashed in those hazel eyes, and the crack she'd thought had healed from Clint's death splintered through her heart. Adan didn't deserve this. He'd risked his life for her and Mazi. He'd given them a place to stay, made them laugh and helped them lick their wounds. "Adan, I'm sorry if I led you on. You deserve—"

"Don't do that." He shook his head. "You don't know what I deserve or how far I'm willing to go to get it. You don't know how every time I look at you, every time I look at Mazi, it hurts. Not just because I'm reminded of my failure to keep Clint alive but because I know I could make you happy. Both of you. If you'd give me the chance."

His conviction wedged under her skin and made her believe. He could make them happy. She had no doubt about that, but moving on, leaving Clint behind… "I can't. I'm sorry."

"Okay." Adan nodded. "As soon as your department has Fischer and the shooter in custody, I'll leave. You won't hear from me again."

Every cell in her body protested that statement. For Mazi's sake. For hers. He'd been exactly what they'd needed to get through this. A rock, a protector, a friend. Hope embodied. But what else was she supposed to do? "I think that's best."

"I'm going to grab a few minutes of fresh air." He hiked his thumb over his shoulder. "Lock the door and arm the system behind me."

She didn't have anything to say to that. Of course he didn't want to be in the same room as her. Let alone the same house. Heavy footsteps echoed down the hallway at his retreat. The front door clicked shut. She secured the door and armed the system as he'd asked. She wasn't just locking him out of the house. She was locking him out of her life, and the dam of tears she'd held back rushed to escape. Hot streaks chased down her face.

"Mommy?" Mazi's small voice shook.

"Yeah, baby?" She swiped the tears away before turning toward her daughter. And froze.

Mazi wasn't alone.

Fischer hugged Mazi against his side, raised his gun and took aim. At Isla. "Disarm the system and unlock the door."

Isla took a step forward. "You son of a—"

"Nuh-uh-uh." He turned the gun on Mazi. "Disarm the system and unlock the front door, or Mazi here is going to have a new ear piercing."

Nausea churned in her gut as she considered her options. Disarm the system to let more of Fischer's men inside or fight a man willing to hurt a child alone. Putting Mazi's life in more danger. She backed toward the front door, keeping her attention on Fischer. "You were watching. Waiting for the system to go down."

"I was very sorry to hear about you and Sarge." Fischer pushed Mazi toward the door in rhythm to each of Isla's steps. "I always thought you two made a good couple. Better than the worthless bastard you married."

Isla's gaze cut to Mazi. Her daughter's bottom lip quavered, and Isla wanted nothing more than to make this all go away. She entered in the six-digit code to the alarm system, and the light on the panel turned from red to green. "Where is he?"

"Don't worry. Sarge won't hear your screams." Fischer flicked the barrel at her again. "Unlock the door. Nice and slow."

She faced the door and moved to twist the dead bolt. Her injured arm was within reaching distance of one of the kitchen drawers, her service piece inside. Could she move fast enough? Would Fischer focus on her if a shootout broke out or would he hurt Mazi first? Whatever the case, Isla had the feeling she wasn't getting out of this unharmed. But Mazi would. No matter the cost. She'd save her daughter. "She doesn't have anything to do with this. She's just a child. I found your shipment. Let her go, and I'll take you to it."

"Now, why would I give up a perfectly good piece of leverage?" Fischer asked.

"Because I think you know what would happen if

you hurt her." She didn't have to fill in the blanks. As much as she wanted to separate her life from Adan's, he'd hunt down every man in Fischer's organization and tear them apart if something happened to Mazi. "The shipment is being held in evidence lockup at the station. I can get you in, but you have to let her go."

Mazi's whimpers cut straight through her.

"I think I'll take my chances, Vachs." Old floorboards protested under Fischer's weight, giving away his position behind her. "Now stop stalling. Unlock the damn door."

"It's your funeral." Isla hinged the dead bolt free and lunged for the kitchen drawer. A bullet ripped past her ear as she pulled her sidearm free. She turned and took aim. "Beetlejuice!"

Mazi knew just what to do. Her daughter ducked and ran as fast as she could for the back bedroom as Isla pulled the trigger. Fischer caught the first bullet in the chest. He stumbled back. His gun fell. Isla pulled the trigger again. Then again. Each time, the soldier who'd threatened her daughter jerked back. Then hit the floor.

The front door burst open.

Only she wasn't fast enough.

The Viking who'd chased her down in the desert ripped the gun free from her grip. He swung his fist into her face. Lightning and a fresh round of tears struck behind her eyes as she slammed into the back of the couch. Digging her fingers into the fabric, she tried to stay upright.

The Viking advanced. She had to give Mazi time to escape out the back window. He cocked his elbow back again, and Isla dropped to the floor. She kicked him straight between the legs and got exactly what she'd hoped for. He crumpled on the spot.

"Mazi." She jumped over Fischer's body and raced for the back bedroom. The window was open. Her daughter had gotten out. Isla threaded one leg through the frame as fast as she could. She knew the area well enough for her and Mazi to get some distance. Pulling free of the window, she searched for Mazi, gun in hand.

The butt of a gun slammed into the side of her head.

And the world went black.

Four shots.

The sound punctured through the mess of emotion ruling his thoughts. Adan shoved to his feet. The tracks he'd found in the woods behind the property were fresh. "Isla."

He raced back toward the house. Branches and leaves scratched at his face, but they wouldn't slow him down. An engine growled in the distance, and he picked up the pace. No. Uneven terrain threatened to trip him. He only pushed himself harder. The wound in his shoulder screamed with every movement until he burst through the tree line.

Two jeeps kicked up dirt behind them as they sped away from the house. The front door had been busted open. Why hadn't the security system alerted his phone? He curved to chase after the vehicles. Isla and Mazi were in those cars. Unpocketing his phone, he dialed the station.

"Nine-one-one, what's your emergency?"

He barely recognized Macie Barclay's voice over the pound of his footsteps and deep breathing. "Macie, they've got them. They took Isla and Mazi. Two jeeps, headed north. They're after the cash. Tell Ford they're coming." He listed off the license plates just as adrenaline failed him. He wasn't strong enough to keep up. Wasn't strong enough to fight for the two ladies he loved. "I'm going after them."

A small imprint of a hand pressed against the second jeep's back window. He couldn't see her face, but he knew Mazi saw him just before the landscape rose and the jeep descended down the hill.

"No. Stay where you are. I'm sending an officer to you." Macie yelled to someone there at the station, but he couldn't make out the words with her hand wrapped around the mouthpiece of her headset. "Don't do this alone, Sergeant. Wait there."

Wait? He'd been waiting. He'd waited to see if Isla and Mazi needed him. He'd waited for Clint to die in his arms. He'd come to Battle Mountain and waited for Isla to heal from her grief. He'd waited too long to get her out of harm's way and had paid the price. He'd waited for her to realize he was there for her. All this waiting, and where had it gotten him? "They're my life now, Macie. I can't wait."

He disconnected the call, jogging back to the house.

There were too many back roads out here, and Fischer and his men had come prepared. They'd shoot him the moment they spotted his vehicle on their tail. Didn't matter. He knew exactly where they were headed. Adan slowed at the large footprint positioned near the dead bolt and shoved through the front door. Someone had kicked the damn thing in. He checked the alarm panel history. Disarmed. With Isla's code. She'd let them inside? No. She never would've put Mazi in that kind of danger. She would've only done it by force. Which meant the bastards had most likely threatened Mazi to get her to cooperate.

Damn it.

He never should've left them alone in the house. He should've known Fischer had been waiting for Adan to let his guard down, and Adan hadn't disappointed. He followed the hallway to Mazi's room, and his gut clenched. The window was open.

One of them had waited for Adan to leave and come in through the window, after the alarm panel had been disarmed. He mentally cataloged the ruffled bedspread, the nightstand light knocked over. All evidence of a struggle. Mazi had fought back against a man three times her size.

And Isla… He'd heard her lock the door behind him.

He retraced his steps to the front of the house. She

wouldn't have heard anything from here. Especially if one of the men had kept Mazi from crying out. Fischer must've surprised her. The kitchen drawer closest to the door was open.

And there was a bullet lodged in the window frame above the sink. She'd gone for her weapon. There'd been an exchange of fire. "You shot him." Four shots. One right after the other, then two more. One had gone into the wall, and the other three must've hit someone. He searched the old hardwood. A black scuff mark angled into the hallway. And there, right beside it, a spatter of smeared blood. "If you were standing here, he was standing…there."

Adan made the shape of a gun with one hand. Isla hadn't been the one shot. She'd hit her target three times. He could give in to the relief, or he could figure out how to get her and Mazi back. "Good girl."

But it hadn't been enough. Someone had come through the front door and evened the playing field. Considering the size of the footprint on the front door, he bet the Viking had survived their tussle in the middle of the desert two nights ago and managed to work his way out of police custody. Which meant Fischer had been the one to grab Mazi.

That last thought stabbed through him so fast, he hadn't been prepared for the onslaught of pain that came with it. His best friend had died because of him. Isla had been put in a sniper's crosshairs because of him. She and Mazi had been taken because of him. He surveyed the house he'd envisioned as part of his plan to keep them safe.

He'd failed them all.

He hadn't kept his word to Clint, and he'd lost Isla and Mazi at the first break in his focus. No wonder she hadn't deemed him worthy enough to be part of their lives. He wasn't.

He'd thought losing his best friend in the middle of an operation had been the lowest point in his life. He was wrong. Mazi and Isla were out there. They were terrified of losing one another.

But he'd bring them home.

No matter the cost.

Adan centered himself in front of the fireplace. He hadn't done much work to this place, but there was one feature he'd spent weeks installing. He hit the hidden button between the second and third bookshelf against the wall, and a panel popped free above the fireplace. Opening the cavity, he dragged a duffel bag identical to the one he and Isla had uncovered at the house in the desert free. The only difference? This one carried his artillery, cash and clothes. He hauled the go bag over his uninjured shoulder and collected a long case from the cavity.

He'd sworn never to use this case or what was inside it after Clint had died and his discharge had been granted, but now it seemed the life he'd left behind would be the only thing to save Isla and Mazi.

Fischer's organization had already proven they were well armed and well recruited. But if there was one thing they didn't have, it was the best sniper in the country. Him. Their shooter had skills, but they weren't anything compared to Adan's. Neither was his conviction.

He dragged both the case and his bag to his car.

The girls had been taken approximately ten minutes ago. Time to move. He rounded to the driver's side of his pickup, started the engine and fishtailed down the road.

Battle Mountain had been through a nonstop criminal wave over the past year. The people of this town needed officers willing to step into the line of fire for them over and over again. They needed Isla. Losing her would cost this place something they couldn't afford. She'd spent her entire professional life in the service of others, spent her marriage supporting a military career, spent the past eight years raising the wildest and most intelligent kid Adan had ever had the honor of knowing. Everything she'd done had been for others. She was love and sharing and friendship incarnate.

And he loved her.

He'd known it the moment before that bullet had found her side two months ago, and he hated himself for it. For what it meant. That every barbecue, every ride to and from the airport, every Sunday dinner and game night, every text message checking in on him—years of generosity—had been building while Clint had still been alive.

He'd fallen in love with his best friend's wife.

Not the idea of her or the life she and Clint had built together or the family they'd raised.

He'd fallen for Isla.

Her patience, her ability to make him see positive qualities in himself he'd sworn didn't exist, her possessive, warm heart. All of it. She was strong—stronger than him—and loving and kind. And she'd been right to kick him out of her life. Because he was nothing compared to her. He never would be.

Adan stripped out of the arm sling and tossed it into the passenger-side seat. A flurry of pink and purple stars swept across his lap. He pried one from his jeans and held it at eye level, his attention cutting from the road. Mazi's confetti.

Every day to that kid had been a day worth celebrating with glitter, and while he'd initially cringed at the thought of vacuuming it out of every nook and cranny in the house, he'd give anything to wake up to another face full of confetti and Mazi's smile. He swung the pickup toward downtown.

Fischer and his men wouldn't go straight to the department for the cash. BMPD knew the bastard's face. He'd send Isla in to retrieve the shipment Clint had stolen, which meant keeping Mazi elsewhere as leverage. From his initial study of Battle Mountain, there were still a few buildings in the town's limits that hadn't been renovated after the bombing six months ago. Fischer would most likely set up in one of them. Close enough to the station but far enough away to avoid recognition and a full-on police bust. "I'm coming, ladies. I'm going to bring you home."

Macie had been right about one thing. He couldn't do this alone. Unpocketing his phone, he scrolled through the numbers he'd saved in case of emergency. There were only two men Adan trusted to have his back against a verified military hit squad. He found the name he wanted and hit dial. He couldn't cover two locations at once. His guess, Fischer would stay with Mazi, and the shooter would keep tabs on Isla. Either way, Adan needed backup. A lot of it.

The line connected. "Don't recall giving you my number, Sergeant."

"Lieutenant." Adan's voice instantly found that edge between respect and duty. "Fischer and his men took Isla and Mazi. I need your help getting them back."

Easton Ford didn't hesitate. "Tell me what you've got in mind."

Chapter Thirteen

How many times could someone get hit in the head before permanent damage set in?

She should know that.

Isla groaned as she pried her head away from what felt like a cinderblock wall. It was dark. The floor was cold. Consciousness hurt like hell, but the alternative was far more frightening. Where was she? The space was big, empty. Windows had been boarded up, barely letting in an outline of light. She could hardly see two feet in front of her. Pain ricocheted through her head as the cuffs around her wrists screeched against some kind of metal plumbing coming out of the wall. No sign of the men who'd taken her from the safe house. No sign of... Her heart shot into her throat. "Mazi?"

A whimper registered from the opposite side of the room. Too far away for her to make out clearly. "Mommy?"

"Oh, baby. It's okay. We're going to get out of this.

All right?" Isla tried to get her feet under her. "Are you hurt?"

"Mommy, I want to go home." Mazi's broken, scared voice hurt her heart. A similar scrape of metal on metal echoed off the corners of the room. Had they cuffed Mazi, too?

"I know. We will. When this is all over, we're going to go home. I promise." Isla licked a split in the bottom of her lip. Her body was still trying to heal from the last time she'd gone up against Fischer and his shooter. Who knew what would happen this time. "Mazi, did they hurt you?"

"No." Her daughter's voice wavered. "But the mean man, the one you shot, he said he's coming back."

Fischer. He'd survived. How was that possible? Unless he'd been wearing a vest. Hell, she should've shot him in the head before he'd had the chance to come near her daughter. One of his men must've grabbed Mazi when she'd gone out the window. Damn it, she should've been there. "I'm not going to let that happen. Understand me? I'm going to get you out of here."

Isla repositioned her feet under her, pulled her hands as far apart as they'd go and shoved away from the wall with everything she had. The cuffs wouldn't budge. Pressure in her chest aggravated the bruises along her sternum, and the force threatened to tear her new stitches free. She took a break, but she wouldn't stop. Not until she and Mazi were as far as they could get from this place.

Voices filtered through one of the boarded windows.

"I know you're scared, but I need you to stay quiet. Okay? They want Mommy. Not you, so I need you to be strong for both of us." Isla swallowed the taste of dust and mildew and fire. "Can you do that?"

The door off to her left wrenched inward before Mazi had a chance to answer.

Isla pressed herself against the wall. Sunlight angled through the doorframe and crawled up her body.

"Well, well, well, look who's finally awake." Fischer stepped into the room. She caught two other men stationed outside the door. That probably meant another two at the opposite exit. The soldier dragged his heels as he closed the distance between them. Crouching in front of her, he slid one calloused hand down her jawline, but fisted his hand in her hair when she tried to back away. Fischer pulled her hair hard enough to expose her throat. "I've never met a woman who tried to punch me full of holes. I gotta admit, it's kind of hot. No wonder those boys got so wrapped up in you. I bet you drove them wild. Always just out of reach."

Whatever boys he was talking about, she didn't care.

"You have me." Her jaw ached under the pressure of trying to swallow with her head tipped back so far. "You can let my daughter go and still walk away after you collect the cash."

His low rumble of a laugh filled the room, and she caught another whimper from Mazi. Stay strong. She had to stay strong. Keep the focus on her and not on Mazi. Fischer shoved her back, releasing his hold in her hair. "You've got more guts than most of the men I served beside, but you're not the one I came to get."

Fischer stood, keeping his gaze on her as he walked backward to the other side of the room.

"What?" Isla's brain raced to connect the dots. He was going to take Mazi. Panic and a healthy dose of desperation had her pulling against the plumbing again. In vain. It wouldn't budge. Not even a centimeter, and it was the only thing keep her from getting to her daughter. "No. No. Please. She has nothing to do with this. She can't help you."

That now-familiar metal grind drowned under Mazi's cries. "Mommy!"

"Sure, she can. Who better to get our shipment from the police station than someone they won't shoot?" Fischer dragged Mazi into the sunlight by one arm. "What's that quote? The one about them being little but fierce. I have complete trust she'll do exactly what we say when we say it, and she probably won't try to shoot us in the process."

"No!" Isla shoved to her feet.

Fischer unholstered his pistol.

"You don't want to go through this all again, now,

do you? Like I told Sarge in the desert. Clint took something from us. We can't let that slide. So you and my new friend here are going to help me make sure no one steps out of line again. Cause if they do…" He pressed Mazi against one side of his body. "Well, you get the idea. Don't worry. Mazi and I are just going to walk into the station and get our shipment. I'll take good care of her while you take the time to think about what happens if you call for help or try to get anyone's attention while you're here."

She didn't need time to think about what that meant. She and Mazi weren't ever going to get the chance to identify Fischer and his men. They'd be dead by the end of their operation. There was an upside, though. She and Mazi would at least get a front-row seat to their violent deaths from heaven once Adan caught up with them. "I hope you get everything that's coming to you, Fischer."

"Believe me, I plan on it." The soldier directed Mazi out the door. "Say bye to Mom, Mazi. You and I are going to take a field trip."

Mazi looked back under Fischer's arm, his pistol just behind her head, and any hope Isla had relied on over the past few days shattered.

"It'll be okay, baby. You'll see." She couldn't let Mazi see her break. Not yet. "I'll be fine here. Go. Do what they tell you to do and come back to me. And, Mazi." Her daughter looked at her. "I love you."

"Ain't that sweet?" Fischer nudged Mazi forward and slammed the door behind them.

Isla was cast back into darkness, but she'd gotten a good lay of the room while the door had been open. This had to be one of the buildings slated for reconstruction after the bombing on Main Street six months ago. She wasn't sure which one of four, but at least she had an idea of where she was and how far she was from the police station. "You've survived worse."

She twisted her wrists, still bruised and scraped from the rope the shooter had used to hang her from that tree, and gripped a cuff in each hand. She pressed her feet into the wall on either side of the plumbing and pulled with everything she had. The hole in her arm screamed a split second before something popped. Her frustrated scream bounced off the cinder-block walls. "Come on!"

Mazi needed her. But the past few days had stripped her down to nothing. Physically, mentally, emotionally. It was only when she was with Adan that she'd felt something more than hopelessness and an empty cavern in her chest.

Had he realized they'd been taken? Would he keep his word after she'd gutted their friendship less than a day ago?

Tears burned in her eyes as she tried the cuffs again. All he'd done for Mazi and her was love them, and she'd gotten scared. No matter how many times she'd wanted to feel desired and important to someone again, she'd pushed him away. She'd given in to the guilt that had followed her around since the moment Clint had been lowered into the grave. But that wasn't what her husband would've wanted. And finding a little piece of happiness—maybe with Adan—wouldn't erase the memories she and Clint had made together. How could she have been so blind?

It wasn't about rewriting or forgetting the past. It had to be about living the present. Adan was her present, and somehow over the past few days, she'd fallen in love with him. Clint hadn't been able to warn her before his death about what was coming, but he'd loved her and Mazi enough to assign a protector over their lives, someone to watch out for and care for them. Maybe that had been his way of telling her it would be okay. She would always love him for trying to look out for them until his last breath. No matter what the evidence said.

The connector between the cuffs groaned.

Then snapped.

Isla fell back onto her rear with a hard thud. She was free to find Mazi and Fischer. Rubbing at her wrists, she watched for movement outside the back door through which her daughter had been taken. She'd seen two guards posted outside when the door was open. Her best chance was another exit. She backed toward the door on the other end of the building, presumably the one that led right into the street.

Debris threatened to give away her plan to surprise whoever was on the other side, but the longer she stayed a hostage, the greater the chance that Mazi would get hurt.

She pried a corner of plywood away from the front window to get a view of the situation outside. A couple ran into the building across the street. A piece of trash flittered by. Main Street was strangely empty for the middle of a workday. Like it had been evacuated. Or another shelter-in-place order had gone into effect. She caught sight of a mass of muscle with his back to the door. The Viking. How he'd wrangled himself free of police custody, she didn't know, but there was no way she was getting through him on her own.

Isla searched the debris left over from the fire. One of Fischer's men had taken her gun after knocking her out, but a long piece of metal could work just as well in a pinch. She slid what looked like a bracket or a brace that had come free from one of the windows and hefted it over one shoulder. Taking position by the front door, she forced herself to not to consider what came next. This was for Mazi. "Bills, I need you. I need your help."

Seconds distorted into a full minute.

"Bills, please. I'm bleeding. I think I tore my stitches. I can't get it to stop." She added a sob at the end, and her target shouldered inside.

Isla swung the brace as hard as she could.

BATTLE MOUNTAIN PD had gotten as many civilians off the street as they could, but that still left the matter of an undermanned police department against what was left of Fischer's entire organization and whoever had sent the shooter to clean up the mess. Wind whistled low over the rooftop where he'd taken position, his rifle butting up against his injured shoulder socket. Adan pressed his finger into the earpiece lodged in his canal. "Any movement?"

"Two guys posted at the back. Both heavily armed and vested." Easton's voice cracked with static. "I think I know one of them. Figures. He was always a jerk I wanted to punch in the face any time I had to talk to him. Lucky for him that wasn't often."

"Small world," Gregson said.

Adan caught a glimpse of Gregson, who was holed up in a crappy sedan down the street, far enough from the station to not raise Fischer's suspicion.

"Not sure I've ever run into anyone I served with by coincidence. Especially in a place like this." The former bomb squad technician took a drink of his soda.

"Not really," Easton said. "There are only a couple dozen or so guys trained in this kind of work and willing to betray everything they believe in for a payout. You can pick them out without even trying nowadays. Suckers don't even try to hide it."

"Mercenaries." Adan pressed his eye against the scope and angled his rifle down the length of Main

Street. If there were two guards posted at the back door, why had Fischer only assigned the Viking to the front? Isla had more than shown her ability to take care of herself. Or was it because Fischer had been counting on something else? Something they couldn't see yet?

He scanned the surrounding rooftops for the shooter. Montrose police had arrived on the scene and started setting up barricades around the police station. They'd have their own sniper in place within a few minutes. And there was the mayor, camera-ready and practically vibrating.

"I got something here." Easton's voice dripped with tension.

Adan's heart rate picked up. He couldn't get a solid view of the alley behind the stretch of buildings. "What's going on?"

"Fischer. He's leaving out the back," Easton said. "He's got Mazi with him. She doesn't look injured or distressed, but he's got a pistol on her. They're heading down the alley toward the station. Son of a bitch is probably going to try to use her as a shield. Force his way into evidence lockup, get what he wants, use her again on the way out. Weston's ready at the station, but we don't want Mazi getting hurt in the crossfire. Want me to put one in his head now?"

Adan's gut clenched. He liked to think Fischer wouldn't hurt an eight-year-old, but how much trust could he put into something like that? He kept the rifle in place. As much as he wanted to end this now, he couldn't put Mazi through something like a man dropping dead beside her without his head attached. "No. We don't know where Isla is or if Fischer has a plan in place to get rid of her in case he's taken out."

"No sign of her out back..." Static cut off Easton's communication for a second. "She must still be inside."

"They'll need to keep in touch in case something goes wrong." Gregson leaned forward in the driver's seat a couple blocks away. "If they've got radios—"

Confusion ripped Adan from his scope. He pressed his earpiece deeper into his ear. "Gregson, repeat."

No answer. He'd trained for situations exactly like this and run a dozen exercises to compensate. He swiveled his attention to Gregson down the street, who'd gotten out of the car. The bomb technician walked a few steps, shaking his head as he pointed to his ear. Their communications had been shut down. Hell. Adan set his eye against the scope.

The Viking.

Where the hell was he? Had he gone inside the building? Had something gone wrong on Fischer's end? What the hell was happening down there?

Gregson couldn't rush the door without giving away their presence. Easton would be outmanned in an instant, and they didn't even know who else was inside with Isla. If she was there at all. Moving Mazi could've been a distraction, a way to split their focus. That left him. Adan hauled his rifle from his perch and slipped along the rooftop, careful to keep low and move fast. He descended the fire ladder on the back of his building and rounded out front.

Gregson was already on the move, heading for the back to assist Easton. It was going down. One way or another he'd bring Isla and Mazi home. Alive. Scanning the street, Adan darted toward the door where the Viking had been posted. The door swung partially inward, revealing nothing but darkness.

Twenty feet. He was almost there.

A glint of metal reflected sunlight out of the corner of his eye.

He pulled up short.

Right before a bullet whizzed past his head.

Adan dove for cover. His rifle hit the asphalt and skidded out of reach as he darted behind a parked vehicle. .30 caliber bullets could cut through a car door, but he wasn't going let one sniper stop him from getting to his girls. Another bullet sliced through the back bumper. He put as much metal between him and the shooter but kept his vantage point through the glass. "Where are you?"

There. The shooter had taken position in what looked like an apartment above one of the Main Street stores across the street. Practically right under Adan's original position. Good sight lines of the front door the Viking had vacated. Terrible for escape. Adan maneuvered around the bumper of the car. A third bullet hit the taillight a few inches from his face. "Three."

Adan picked up a shard of red plastic and angled it around the bumper into the open. It was a risk, but necessary for him to get to his rifle. A fourth bullet snatched it out of his hand. Pain radiated down his forearm from the impact, and he ducked back behind cover. Not a bad shot from less than a hundred yards. "Four."

One more, and the shooter would have to switch magazines, but the sniper had most likely figured out Adan's plan. He shifted to the very edge of the vehicle, nearly out in the open, but the fifth shot never came. The shooter was waiting for the kill shot, the one that would take him out for good.

His breathing registered in his ears. The entire town had gone silent. He couldn't hear anything from inside the building. Was Isla alive? Had his game of cat and mouse already cost him everything? Without comms, there was no way to know the status of Ford or Gregson, either. He was on his own. "Don't disappoint me now."

Adan lunged for his rifle.

Pavement scraped up his knees and elbows as he slapped a hand over the stock. The fifth and final bullet bounced off the asphalt beside his hand. He had five seconds before a reload.

He pressed the butt of the rifle into his wounded

shoulder, set his eye over the scope and pulled the trigger.

Another catch of metal flashed in sunset.

Right before the shooter fell out that second-floor apartment window.

Victory charged through him as the minutes after Clint had been shot played in his head right there in the middle of the street. He hadn't just sworn to watch over Isla and Mazi as his best friend had taken his last breath. He'd sworn to find the shooter who'd taken Clint's life. Adan dragged himself across the street, his rifle heavier than ever before.

The face that had haunted him since he'd found Isla in the desert stared back at him as he approached. A trembling smile hiked one side of the man's mouth higher as blood seeped from the chest wound. The exact spot Clint had been shot. He clutched onto something over his chest, his words barely audible. "You won't win."

The urge to watch the shooter suffer for everything he'd done to the people Adan loved took hold. But he wasn't that man. Clint and Isla and Mazi had shaped him into something better. He grabbed for his phone and hit 911.

No answer.

Adan dialed again as the shooter's hand fell away from his chest, exposing an ornate silver cross. The good luck charm. Nothing on the other end of the line. Fischer must've already breached the station.

And now the shooter was dead.

But this wasn't over.

Adan turned back to the abandoned building across the street, rifle at the ready. He kicked in the front door to the building and forced himself inside. Ready for anything.

Except Isla standing over the Viking's body.

She raised a slim piece of metal up in defense, her expression wild, hair a mess as she moved in to attack.

Adan strapped his rifle over his head and raised both hands in surrender. She'd fought for and won her life. "It's me."

Thin shoulders rose and fell in erratic pulses. She blocked in incoming sunlight with one hand, keeping hold of her makeshift weapon with the other. "Adan?"

Metal hit cement in a burst of ear-piercing reverb as she rushed him. Isla slammed herself against his chest and set her head over his heart. Right where he needed her. "I'm sorry. I didn't know what else to do. He threatened to hurt Mazi if I didn't disarm the system."

"I know. Don't worry. I've got you." Adan secured his arms around her frame, resting his cheek on the crown of her head. "And we're going to get Mazi."

Isla straightened, swiping one hand across her face. "How? Fischer took her to the station. He's going to use her to get the cash. If we go in there—"

"I won't let him hurt her." He backed off, gripping both of her arms in his. The gauze secured around her bullet wound had soaked through. She'd most likely torn the stitches, but heaven help the person who would try to convince her to get help over saving her daughter. Adan had no idea what waited for them inside the police station, but lack of intel hadn't stopped him from carrying out his mission before. He'd trained for this. He was good at this. And nothing would stop him from bringing Mazi home. "Do you trust me?"

The tears dissolved. Her resolve surfaced. In that moment, this wasn't the generous, sincere, warmhearted mother and EMT he'd fallen in love with over the past decade. She'd become a law enforcement officer, ready to take on the world for a single life, and he couldn't stop taking it all in. "What's the plan?"

Chapter Fourteen

"No." The mayor stood a bit taller with the help of his cane.

"What do you mean 'no'?" Isla didn't understand. With Chief Ford inside the station, she and Adan had laid out their plan to the man who called the shots. They were going to get Mazi back. They were going to end this.

"I meant exactly what I said, Officer Vachs." Mayor Higgins ducked out from beneath the tent set up across the street from the police station as a command station. Any and all information about the case went through him, and the power of that fact had seeped into the curve of his old, crooked mouth. "Montrose PD is on the scene as we speak. They've got a team in place, and not a single officer from Battle Mountain PD is to interfere. Do you understand?"

"That's my daughter in there!" Isla stepped into the man determined to take over this town for no other reason than he had the power to do so. Strong hands locked onto both of her arms from behind. "I'm not just going to stand here and wait—"

"Yes, you are, oOfficer. Because right now I'm in charge, and you never should've had a hand in this case seeing as how it's connected to your husband." He pointed a thick, sausage-like finger in her face. "Because of you, we now have a standoff with two officers and two civilians inside, two bodies at the funeral home and an officer on the way to the hospital. The people of this town deserve a police force who can protect them, who don't carry out personal vendettas, so as of this minute, you are officially relieved of duty, Officer Vachs. All of you are. Thank you for your service. Now get off my scene."

"What?" She fought the grip holding her back. If she wasn't a police officer anymore, how was she supposed to get Mazi out of the station? How was she supposed to protect her family? "You can't do that. This town needs us."

"I can, and I just did. If you'll excuse me. I need to clean up the mess you and this department made." The mayor called over his shoulder for an update, and an officer Isla didn't recognize jogged to meet him. Papers rustled over the podium he took position behind.

Adan stepped between her and the mayor. "Three bodies."

"Excuse me?" The mayor was forced to look up at him as Adan straightened to his full height. Tensions ran high as two Montrose officers set their hands on the butts of their weapons.

"There are three bodies connected to this case. The last one is over in the old bookstore down the street." Adan motioned to Isla behind him. "The officer you just relieved of duty? She's the only reason these men haven't slaughtered every single person in this town to get what they want, including you. So you have a choice: reinstate her and the rest of BMPD to save Battle Mountain, or watch Fischer and his men burn this town to the ground all over again."

"Is that a threat?" The lines around the mayor's mouth twitched. He talked a good game, but Isla knew the impression Adan made on people who didn't actually know him. The officers behind the mayor waited for the tipping moment before acting. "I don't know who the hell you are or what you're doing here, friend, but this is a police investigation. I've got a military force tearing apart this town and dropping bodies every chance they get. So if you don't mind, I've got work to do."

"Sir—" The Montrose police captain pushed through the ring of blue set around the mayor. "Our sniper has the suspect in view through a window."

"Then what's the holdup, Captain?" The mayor turned on the officer. "Tell him to put the son of a bitch down before this escalates."

"Sir, it's not a clean shot. The girl he's holding hostage is right in the line of fire," the captain said.

Every cell in Isla's body froze.

"If we let this get any more out of hand, who knows what will be left of this town." The mayor's gaze flickered to her, then away. "I'm sorry, Ms. Vachs, but I have to think about the good of the many. Order him to take the shot."

"No!" Isla wrenched free of Adan's hold. Or he let her go, she wasn't sure which. It didn't matter. They were going to shoot Mazi. Fire and rage and grief tornadoed through her until she couldn't tell where her hurt for Clint's death ended and fear for her daughter's life began. She shoved Higgins out from behind the podium. "That's my daughter! You can't do this! She's just a child!"

The mayor fell back, his cane failing him, and landed on his backside. Montrose police closed in, barricading her from getting to him. One officer moved to hinge her arms behind her back, but she wouldn't stop fighting. Not until Mazi was safe in her arms.

"Touch her, and you'll lose that arm." Adan stepped between her and an entire flank of police, his voice dipping into dangerous territory. "Understand?"

The officers seemed to take in his size and thought better of attacking a woman fearing for her child.

"She just assaulted me, damn it. Get them out of here!" Mayor Higgins pointed up at Isla. "That's an order."

"I'm begging you, Captain. Please." Isla focused on the police force from Montrose. "Do not let your sniper take that shot. Please. That's my daughter."

"You better get out of here," the captain said.

The Montrose officers motioned for Isla and Adan to leave the area. One rounded behind Isla as she struggled get through the mayor's thick head. "This isn't about sacrificing one life for the good of the many, and you know it. Your investigation, what you're doing here—it's nothing but your ego, and the people of this town will figure out exactly what kind of man you are when this is over. You can count on it."

"Tell him to take the shot, Captain," the mayor said. "The rest of you get them out of here!"

Isla tried to shove through the blue line pushing her back. "No!"

The mayor dismissed her without another thought.

Adan slipped his hand between her ribs and arm, directing her away from the command center.

"What are you doing?" Betrayal and a flare of resentment coursed through her veins as she tried to pry his grip loose. "I'm not leaving. They're going to shoot Mazi."

"And we can't help her from here," he said.

A thread of confusion tangled in her thoughts. He was right. The mayor wasn't going to change his mind. Because this wasn't about public safety. This was a publicity stunt, a way to show Battle Mountain that they'd been right about the department all along. She only hoped whatever shooter Montrose PD had supplied would hesitate to pull the trigger with an eight-year-old bystander in the way of his target. Adan directed her between two parked cars along Main Street and into Caffeine and Carbs. "If you think pastries are going to make me feel better, you've—"

He kept her moving, past the pastry cases, past Reagan and the surprise etched into his expression, through the back of the building and outside. Adan scanned the length of the alley as though he was looking for someone.

Movement registered from about ten feet away.

"You heard all that?" Adan asked.

A dark outline stepped into view, and Isla stopped fighting.

Easton Ford, in all his glory, holstered his weapon.

"Every word. Mayor Higgins won't be able to argue about his order to have an eight-year-old shot come election time. Officer Vachs, good to see you in one piece." Easton nodded in that overly gentlemanly way career soldiers tended to adhere to. He then turned his attention back to Adan.

"Where's Gregson?" Adan asked.

"Took one in the leg before putting those two bastards' lights out. I've got them both secured down in the old bookstore. Believe me, I'd rather face another IED before telling Alma what went down."

Easton's gaze bounced between the two of them. "What's the plan?"

Adan looked down at her in expectation.

He was the strategist. He was the one who'd trained for this kind of situation, and she trusted him to keep his word. But he wanted her to decide how to get her daughter back, and she fell a bit more in love with him right then. Though now wasn't the time to voice her regret about cutting him out of their lives. Isla licked her busted lip, the pain keeping her in the present. This wasn't about what had happened. It wasn't about what would happen. All that mattered was what was she going to do now to get Mazi back. "How can you get me inside that station?"

"I've got an inside man. Well, I've got Macie." He whistled low. Three notes cut through the uncertainty and doubt circling Isla's mind. The glass back door of the station cracked open. "After your call into the station, she warned Weston what was coming. He had her take up in one of the cells, posing as a drunk. Behind bars, she isn't much of a threat in a hostage situation. With a key, she can get you inside."

Isla couldn't wait any longer. They had a way in, and she was going to take it.

Easton tried to keep up with her. "You can't just go barging in there, Vachs. From what Macie's been able to get to me, Weston and Fischer are in a standoff in the bullpen. With Mazi in the middle. These guys are military. Fischer will have accounted for every variable before he even stepped foot in the building."

"He didn't account for me." This was Mazi they were talking about. There were no rules. Not when it came to bringing her daughter home. She turned back just before hiking the three cement steps leading to the back door. "Give me a gun."

Easton cast a questioning glance at Adan, who nodded. Adan handed off his rifle to the former Green Beret and accepted two pistols, giving one over to Isla.

"You know how to use a rifle?" Adan asked.

"Spent some time in the sandbox with a sniper for a few weeks." Easton racked a load and pointed the weapon at the ground, setting his eye over the scope. "How hard can it be?"

She checked the magazine of her weapon. Three shots left. It wasn't much, but it would have to work. Everything she'd fought for since Clint's death, everything she and Mazi had been through—it had all been leading to this. To her protecting her family. "Thank you."

"Don't thank me yet." Easton shouldered the rifle, scanning the rooftops. "You still have to survive what's coming."

Isla slipped through the door ahead of him.

They stayed low and moved slow so as not to arouse Fischer's attention. One wrong move and it would be over. They had to play by the rules here. Anything outside the lines could get Mazi killed.

Macie Barclay slid into view from the back room. She hugged a duffel bag to her chest. Her hands shook as she crouched beside them. Anyone looking down the hall would see them at the back door, but Fischer and Weston Ford seemed to be keeping each other distracted. For now.

Voices carried down the hallway and into the back of the building. Shouts and something else. Crying. He noted the exact moment Isla recognized Mazi's whimpers. She hesitated, almost as though warring with herself. Should she follow the plan, or should she race to save her daughter? Adan settled a hand on her shoulder, and she visibly released the tension down her back.

He turned to Macie.

"Get that to Easton outside. No one else. Understand? Not the mayor. Not Montrose PD." He waited for a sign Macie hard heard him. She nodded. "He's waiting for you out back."

"Okay." The dispatcher latched on to his partner's arm. "Be careful. That man… He'll kill all of us if he gets the chance. And you"—Macie turned bright eyes onto him "—they better make it out of this, or I'll curse your manhood to rot and turn green."

He believed every ounce of her conviction. "I promise."

Isla set her hand over Macie's. "Go. We'll see you on the other side."

Macie shouldered through the glass door slowly, then slid through its opening.

The door closed with a thud.

The dispatcher centered herself in the glass, her eyes wide and full of regret.

They'd just lost the element of surprise.

Adan motioned the dispatcher to run as he counted off the seconds. Macie vanished, duffel bag of counterfeit cash in hand. Whatever happened today, Battle Mountain PD would have enough to build a case. Because of her.

Scuffing footsteps registered from down the hall. "Whoever you are, you've got until the count of three to put down your weapons and get to this room before I put another bullet in the chief here."

Another? Isla looked back at Adan, silently questioning.

Adan stood, weapon in hand.

Panic infused Isla's gaze. She shook her head, then craned it down the hall to get a view of Fischer. She kept her voice to a whisper. "What are you doing?"

"I'm going out there," he said.

Isla shot to her feet, dragging him against her. "You don't have to do this. We can figure out another way—"

"One," Fischer said.

"Yes, I do. I gave you my word, Bugs." He swiped

a tendril of hair out of her face to see her better. "Before I came to Battle Mountain, I'd lost everything. But you and Mazi blindsided me when I least expected it. I'm not just doing this because of Clint. I'm doing this because I don't want a future without either of you in it."

"Two." Another whimper escaped Mazi's throat.

They couldn't stop time. They couldn't stop Fischer from killing anyone else, but Adan could sure as hell slow the bastard down. Long enough to give her and Mazi a chance to escape. To finally start living their lives.

Isla crushed her mouth to his.

He let himself enjoy one last taste of her, then pulled away and handed off his weapon. He wouldn't need it. "No matter what happens, I need you to get Mazi out."

"I will. Just…" She handled both weapons. "Come back to me, Sergeant."

Five words seared through his heart and armored him with the clarity to face what was coming. Two deployments, dozens of training exercises and years of violence and war—nobody had ever waited for him to come home. But Isla did. That in and of itself was worth fighting for. Adan nodded, stepping out into the hall.

Fischer kept his gun centered on something—or someone—out of Adan's line of sight. Most likely the chief. But his grip around Mazi's small frame tightened. "I take it Cervantes is dead."

"Is that the guy who shot Isla a couple months back, then tried again a few days ago?" Adan measured his steps carefully. Not too fast. Not too slow. If he was going to give Isla an opening to Mazi, he had to time it just right. As long as she made her way down the opposite hallway leading to the chief's office, he'd have Fischer's full attention. "If that was the best sniper your new friends had, you're screwed. I mean, at least send a guy who can count his rounds in the middle of a firefight."

"He was good enough for Clint, Moore, White, Burgess and that old lady, but you're right. I guess a winning streak can't last forever." Anger simmered in those dark eyes Adan had once trusted to have his back. "So this is, what, Sarge? The last showdown?"

"If that's what you want. You okay, Maz?" Her small nod gave him a bit of hope. She was a real trouper. Stronger because of what she'd already been through. Adan took another step, forcing Fischer to turn the gun on him. He only hoped Weston Ford wouldn't take the opportunity to shoot with Mazi still in the crossfire. His girl looked at him with panic and fear and desperation. She wanted him to take her home, and he would. Just as soon as Fischer was in cuffs. "It's over. The cash is long gone. You're outnumbered, outgunned. Battle Mountain PD will build a case and round up anyone left in your organization. There's no way out of this for you. Either you face the people you pissed off or you surrender to Chief Ford there. Which is it going to be, Fischer? Cuffs or a body bag?"

"You're trying to convince me my shipment just left the building on its own? That's your play, Sarge?" Fischer motioned to the other side of the room. "Then what's that Chief Ford has got?"

He stepped into the main bullpen. Hell.

Weston Ford kept his pistol raised on Fischer, but it was only a matter of time before the chief dropped it and was forced to give Fischer free rein to kill them all. The man's hand shook as blood spread across his button-down. Gunshot wound. He'd set himself against one of the desks, a black duffel bag behind him, but the chief could keel over any minute. "Sergeant, don't suppose you brought an EMT with you?"

Ford's question hit with double meaning.

Adan cut his gaze to the hallway behind the younger Ford, giving away Isla's position, but with her chief bleeding out in front of her, given the choice, she wouldn't be able to pass Ford over to grab for Mazi.

She could only choose one life to save.

He had to be the one to get Mazi out of here. To do that, he had to go through Fischer.

A low laugh rumbled through Fischer's chest. "You never were one to look at the whole picture. Just the small target in front of you. That's the problem with you snipers. You're great at shooting to kill on the battlefield, but real life isn't just about playing God, Sarge." The soldier shook his head, amused. "Even if you kill me, *Sangre por Sangre* will take that fake cash. They'll finish what we started. They'll come for Mazi here. They'll kill Isla right in front of you, and there won't be anything you can do to stop them."

"In that case, I guess I'll just have to make it real clear they're not welcome in Battle Mountain. By using you as an example." Adan wasn't going to wait for Fischer to become desperate for an escape. He was going to take Mazi home now.

"Beetlejuice!" Isla rounded the corner into the bullpen, gun aimed, and pulled the trigger. Her shot went high, as she'd meant, giving Mazi the chance to get out of the way.

"Oh, no, you don't, Mazi." Fischer squeezed Mazi against him, keeping her from moving. He turned his weapon on Isla. "I learned my lesson back at the house. No way you're running from me this time."

Adan tackled the bastard a split second before another gunshot exploded. They hit the floor as one, tangled in a mass of muscle and punches.

Mazi screamed as she struggled to get free of two men trying to dominate each other.

"Maz, go!" Adan shoved her across the floor, out of the soldier's reach.

Fischer's gun slid over tile. Cries pierced Adan's

focus as Mazi ran for her mother. Fischer took his distraction for the advantage it was and slammed his fist into the side of Adan's head. Both Ford and Isla were collecting Mazi and maneuvering her down the hall.

"Where do you think you're going?" Fischer lunged for his weapon and started to follow after them.

A bullet came through the window and lodged in the wall inches from Fischer's head. Glass rained down over Adan's face and neck as a red dot sight moved along the wall toward Isla, Ford and Mazi.

Damn it. The mayor must've ordered the shot.

"Isla, get down!" Adan shucked off the disorientation and went for the nearest weapon. The station's emergency fire ax. Without anything to aim at, the shooter wouldn't pull the trigger. Busting through the glass, Adan gripped the compressed wood as hard as he could as Fischer spun to confront him.

Fischer wouldn't ever stop. The military had trained him too well.

Like they'd trained Adan.

He ran the head of the ax into Fischer's wrist. His teammate dropped the gun a second time. Adan followed the hit up with another ram into the son of a bitch's ribs.

Fischer collapsed to both knees, out of breath, and crumpled to his side. Out of the sniper's sightline. "They'll never be safe, Sarge. You'll never be able to protect them as long as I live. I'll just keep coming. Count on it."

Adan rammed the butt of the ax into the man's temple.

Fischer fell onto his back. Out cold.

"I will." Adrenaline drained faster than he expected, and the ax fell from Adan's grip. It landed with a hard thud as the past few days caught up in an instant. He stared through the window where the shot had originated. A single shooter had taken position on the rooftop across the street but was now pulling his weapon from the ledge.

It was over.

Fischer would spend the rest of his days in a military prison.

Adan rounded the corner to find Mazi crying against the wall. He scooped her into his arms, more solid with her suffocating grip around his neck. "It's okay, Maz. I've got you."

"Come on, Chief. Open your eyes." Isla administered chest compressions to the prone man lying on the floor. She'd compacted her T-shirt and pressed it against the gunshot wound, but it wasn't enough to stop the bleeding. "Don't give up. Chloe will never talk to me again if I let you die."

The back door slammed open.

Adan drew his weapon, taking aim before recognition flared.

Mazi plastered herself against his chest at another possible threat.

"Hell. Macie, get the medics!" Easton Ford didn't bother looking at the gun on him. He only had attention for his brother. He rushed the chief and started dragging Weston from the station as Isla, Adan and Mazi huddled together right there on the blood-stained floor.

Chapter Fifteen

The grave site had been cleaned.

Isla set a fresh bouquet of white carnations beside the headstone. Some of the grass had overgrown near the base, and she plucked it away. Two days since the scene in the station. Two days since she'd nearly lost everything to greedy men who'd already tried to break her. It all seemed like a dream now. Fischer. Grabbing Mazi. Chief Ford's collapse in the hallway. She still hadn't processed it all. Time would be the ultimate truth teller. "This is all your fault, you know."

Letters etched into the headstone blurred with tears.

In memory of Clint Vachs. Lieutenant. US Army. His birthdate and death date followed.

A surge of anger and pain simmered. "You were the one who was supposed to be here, Clint. They came for you, but I guess if you hadn't died overseas, we would've lost you anyway. Fischer would've come for you one way or another. You're lucky they're not burying me next to you, though. I'd haunt you to eternity for what you put us through."

She pulled a folded envelope from her coat pocket.

Macie Barclay had taken the duffel bag of cash and run, but once the bullets had stopped flying and Fischer was arrested, she'd handed off an envelope as Isla and Mazi were getting checked out by her old crew. It had been tucked inside the bag, something she and Adan had missed when they'd discovered the counterfeit cash.

Clint's messy script scrawled across the front. *For Bugs.*

Slipping her fingers beneath the edge, she pulled a single piece of paper from the depths and unfolded it. *"If you're reading this letter, then I'm dead, and I'm sorry. I tried to be the hero you've always seen me as, but in the end, I'm just a man."*

She read through the letter then again. Tears hit the paper and streaked the ink. Clint had manipulated his way into Fischer's organization, he'd arranged the deal with the cartel stateside, stolen the counterfeit cash then hidden it—all in an attempt to bring corrupt soldiers to justice. The cash had been his proof. He'd planned to expose them all. Keeping her on the outside had been his way to ensure she and Mazi wouldn't become targets. *"If my plan doesn't work, trust Adan. He's a pain in the ass, but he'll do whatever it takes to protect you both. I love you with all my heart, Bugs. You made my life."*

Movement out of her peripheral vision eased the emotion lodged in her throat. A warm, strong hand slid across her low back. Adan hugged her into his chest. He was back in the sling, his arm practically useless after the standoff with Fischer. Same as hers after she'd torn the stitches, but he pulled it off dressed in his full ceremonial uniform. She just looked pathetic. "You finally read it."

"Thought this would be the best place." She folded the paper back up. "Then I could yell at him in person."

"Feel better?" Adan bent down to set his hand on top of the headstone. Clearing a single leaf from the base, he angled his head down in respect.

Isla had lost her husband the day Clint had died. Adan had lost his brother. He hurt as much as she did, yet the only thing he wanted to know was how she was doing? She slid the envelope into her jacket pocket. "No. It was easier to be mad at him for getting himself killed when I thought he was part of Fischer's organization. Now that I know he was trying to bring them down from the inside and failed... I just miss him."

"Me, too." Adan straightened. Bruising Rorschached across his strong features, and she gave in to the impulse to try to sweep the coloring away. He leaned into her hand and closed his eyes, and right then she saw what Clint had seen. A protector, a man who would fight against any threat, a soldier who'd never betray his beliefs. Her husband had been right about him. Adan had been the perfect man to carry out Clint's dying wishes.

"I love you." She hadn't had the guts to say those three little words out loud, but with knowing Clint had prepared for her future, for Mazi's future, the guilt and shame she'd carried didn't hold any more weight. She loved her husband. She missed him with every fiber in her being, but the past week had showed her she couldn't spend the rest of her life punishing herself out of some self-imposed extension of her marriage. She'd nearly died. Mazi had been abducted.

It was time to live for now.

Time to appreciate and love the life she'd built on her own. With Adan.

She smoothed her thumb over his battered face. All these bruises, all the pain—it had been for her. "The other day when I said I wanted things to go back the way they were… I was scared. I felt guilty. You spend ten years of your life with someone, have a child with them, it comes with a kind of loyalty after their death. You never plan on outliving your spouse, and all this time I didn't want to face the truth that was my life. I felt I owed him my misery, that I was honoring his memory if I refused to move on. What you said to Mazi about fear only making us stop trying to live our lives, Clint said that to me the day we got engaged, and now I understand. My fear of leaving him behind, of finding something new to live for, hurt more than losing him. But with you—" she stepped into him "—I feel like myself. Like I used to. I feel…ready."

Adan set his hand over her, angling his mouth to kiss her bruised knuckles. "What do you want, Isla?"

There was that question again, the one no one but Adan had the consideration to ask. This time, she knew the answer. "I want you. All of you. The man who threw an ice cream party to make a little girl feel better, the man who smiled when he sat down for one of my big family breakfasts." She slipped her thumb over his bottom lip. "The man who kissed me like I was the only woman in his entire world and treats my daughter as his own."

Adan tugged her against him, covering her mouth with his. Her brain tried to trigger her defensive habits, but her heart…her heart knew better now. It knew him, and she wanted more. "You got it. All of me."

He worked to memorize her from the inside out, and Isla let him. She didn't know what the future held for them, but for once she was okay with not knowing. Life was unpredictable, but if there was one thing she could count on, it was Adan. Nerves swirled through her stomach at the thought of what came next. She hadn't lied before. She was ready. Not just for the physical aspect in their relationship, but to feel wanted again, worthy. Loved. And she wanted to love. She wanted to show him exactly what it felt like to have a partner who had his back. Forever.

"What are you doing?" Mazi's face centered be-

tween them as she stared up. She looked between
Isla and Adan, interest and a whole lot of confusion
lighting up her bright eyes.

Isla set herself fully back on her feet and smoothed
the wrinkles she'd pressed into Adan's collar. The
embarrassment would cling to her every time Mazi
looked at her from now on. Oh, hell. "I lost my gum."

"In Uncle Adan's mouth?" Mazi pulled her own
wad of spearmint gum and offered it over. "Here.
You can borrow mine. I have more."

Adan's low laugh rumbled through her chest still
pressed against his.

Isla accepted her daughter's offering, burying a
cringe. She'd changed her daughter's diapers and
literally caught throw up in her hands when Mazi
had suffered from acid reflux. Gum was a whole
new disgusting adventure. "Thanks, Maz. Why don't
you say goodbye to all the soldiers you met today?"

Hopefully for long enough Isla could get rid of
the gum in her hand without hurting Mazi's feelings.

"I'll bring you back another piece of gum when
I'm done chewing it!" Mazi skipped off between
a thousand other headstones like Clint's, smelling
flowers along the way. It had taken nearly ten minutes to convince her not to bring a handful of confetti, but from the look of it, her daughter had hidden
some in her pockets. Even after everything Mazi
had been through, she hadn't lost her sparkle, and
Isla could only smile for those people who benefited

from it. Like these soldiers and their visiting families. Or maybe Mazi's sparkle was what was saving her from everything she'd been through. Either way, Isla couldn't avoid talking to her daughter about what they'd been through and what would happen for them next.

"You lost your gum?" Adan set her at arm's length. "Sooner or later, we're going to have to tell her the truth."

"Give me a break. I'm new at this." Isla tossed the wad Mazi had lent her and wiped her hands down her uniform. "Just…keep your mouth to yourself until I can put together a semi-coherent discussion."

He smiled at her as though that was one order he didn't intend to follow. "Even after she goes to bed?"

"Well, maybe not then." She threaded her free hand into his with a backward glance at the gravestone dedicated to Clint. The heaviness she expected to follow her never came, and Isla felt as though she could finally breathe. They were safe. Fischer and his men would never come for them again. As for his threat about the cartel, she highly doubted an organization so large would worry about her and an eight-year-old, but whatever happened, she was prepared.

She had her very own personal bodyguard on her side.

Isla pulled Adan to a stop just before they reached her monster truck. She'd had to have the engine block replaced, puzzle the back seat back together and patch a deep bullet hole in the hood, but it ran and looked good as new. Better even. Clint would be proud. "There's one matter we still haven't talked about. I love you, and you love me. I think we made that clear, but our living arrangements—"

"I want you and Mazi to move in with me." He turned to face her, keeping her hand in his. "I'll tear out that old kitchen and get some new furniture. We can redo the grass in the backyard so Mazi has a place to play. We might even be able to fit a bigger dining table in down the road."

"Down the road?" Goose bumps prickled down her arms as she tried to pick apart his words. Her stomach flipped at the idea of waking up beside this man every morning, of going to bed with him every night, of a future together. As a family. "Do you… have plans for down the road?"

"Nothing concrete, but I have a few ideas in mind." He pressed his mouth to hers, and the sizzle she'd felt the first time he kissed her resurrected. "How about it, Officer Vachs? Ready to make a new life together?"

She smiled against his mouth and secured her free hand around the back of his neck. "Waiting on you."

"Mommy! Here's another piece of gum!" Mazi bounded toward her, hand outstretched.

Isla detached herself from Adan and wrenched open the passenger-side door of the truck. "Sorry, Sergeant. You're on your own."

She slammed the door closed just as her daughter tackled Adan gum-hand first.

"Looking good for a dead man, Ford." Adan traced the shaved patch of hair that used to be there above his left ear as he shouldered into the hospital room. Damn gum. He'd have to check Mazi's hands every time she tackled him now. Who knew what else he could lose?

Weston Ford hefted the remote higher to turn off the television. "You made it. I was sure I'd have to send Chloe to Alamosa to get her to leave me on my own for a couple hours. Only way I could get her to go home was tell you her you'd volunteered to look after me. Thanks for not making me a liar."

"Anytime." A quick glance at the screen told him Mayor Higgins was still trying to dig himself out of a bottomless pit. His order to have Montrose police's sniper shoot through Mazi to get his suspect had gone public with the help of an anonymous source at the scene. Funny how that had come out considering there hadn't been any media around.

"Hey, Chief." Isla came in behind him and slid a large vase of flowers and a to-go bag onto the side table beside the bed. "Wasn't sure if you were a rose kind of guy or if you preferred lilies, so we let Mazi pick. You get every color of dahlias Franny's Flowers had in stock."

"Thank you. They're nice." The chief moved the

vase out of the way to get a better look at the to-go bag and smiled. "Is that one of those pastries you like so much? What are they called? Viennas, or something."

Isla snatched the bag she'd left on the table and hugged it like she'd protect it with her life. "*Viennoi-series*. And this one is not for sale. I've had to wait three days to get my hands on this because some-one said I was pushing myself too hard and made me stay home."

"She doesn't share. Believe me, I already tried." Adan rounded the end of the bed and took in the view out the back. Battle Mountain's small clinic was positioned perfectly to see the entire length of Main Street and the police station. "I think Mazi tried once, too. Nearly got her finger taken off."

"It's not that hard to understand. Don't touch my food." Isla took a seat in one of the pleather chairs near the bed and dug into the bag. In seconds, she'd practically melted in place. And, damn, wasn't that the sexiest thing he'd ever seen. Isla at peace, com-fortable with being herself. For once taking into ac-count what she needed rather than putting everyone else ahead of her. It was a beautiful sight to behold. "What's going on here? They treating you all right?"

"I'm fine." Ford leaned back against the pillows propped up behind him. "Would love to see the may-or's face in person when he finds out one of my own officers leaked his order after all the BS he put the department through."

"Oh, come on, now. He's had a hard week. Being removed from office and all." Isla took another bite of her pastry. "Let's give him a couple weeks to calm down. What's going on with Fischer and the men we rounded up at the scene?"

Adan had learned to read this woman better than anyone else over the past week. It if was up to her, she would've arrested Mayor Higgins for child endangerment, misuse of power and anything else she could find to put him behind bars. The son of a bitch was lucky the sniper he'd ordered to take the shot had refused to pull the trigger until Mazi was out of the crosshairs.

"Seems the army got real interested about what happened here, especially all the extracurricular activities Fischer and his guys carried out. Gail Oines's death, shooting Layton Burgess, coming after the two of you. Kendric recovered the bullet used to kill Oines, matched it up real nice with the one left in her son and the one you'd saved on that chain of yours. There's no denying that guy you said was named Cervantes was the shooter who came after you two months ago and again a few days ago after we had the chance to take a look at his rifle. We were able to connect him back to a bunch of hits and assassinations the FBI's been investigating in New Mexico." Ford looked to Isla. "From what I've heard, the military is examining Clint's death again. They've started their own probe into your buddies, Moore and White, too."

"Oh," she said. "Do they think they have a strong enough case to charge Fischer and the soldiers he recruited?"

"Didn't get a chance to ask seeing as how I'm prohibited from moving from this bed. Easton's in contact with the unit that scooped up everyone involved—including the bodies left behind—before we could get them processed. He knows one of their MPs." The chief set a hand over his side. "He told me Fischer was looking to make a deal. Information on the people he was doing business in exchange for leniency."

"The cartel," Adan said. "Sangre por Sangre."

"My contact at the DEA said they're real big in moving counterfeit cash right now," Ford said. "Based out of New Mexico. Brutal. Unforgiving. The feds have been trying to make a case for years, but anyone they can get on the inside turns up dead. Wouldn't be surprised if Fischer and his men ended up as more notches in their belts."

"I still don't understand why this is all happening now," Isla said. "Why wait to come after me when Clint took that shipment more than a year ago?"

"If we get the chance to ask the leader of the cartel who ordered the hit, I'll let you know." Ford's small smile was meant as reassurance, but even Adan understood law enforcement couldn't answer every question that came up during an investigation.

"What about Isla's job?" Adan asked.

"What about it?" Ford tried to shift his weight in the bed, but the look on his face said every movement came with a price. "As soon as Chloe gives you the all clear, you can go back into the field."

Adan set his gaze on Isla.

"I'm not fired?" She lowered the pastry, ignoring the flecks of chocolate on her bottom lip.

"Not that I'm aware of. We need you too damn much." Ford messed with one of the buttons that controlled the bed and ended up raising his feet higher, then lower, then higher again. "You're a good officer. If it weren't for you and your bodyguard here, Fischer would've gutted this town. People know that. Some might blame you for bringing trouble. They might look at you differently now that the dust has settled, but in the end, you did what anyone else would've done. You stood up for your family, and anyone willing to take on an entire rogue military operation to protect this town and the people she loves deserves a spot in my department."

"Fischer said the cartel will keep coming after us." Isla's voice dropped. "You're not worried you and this department will get dragged into another fight?"

A part of Adan realized she hadn't been solely talking to the chief, that she'd posed the question to both of them when her gaze flickered to his. But

Adan had made his choice, and he kept his promises. He wasn't going anywhere.

"Vachs, this town has gone head-to-head with a serial killer and helped my brother take down another. The people here have endured a bombing that took out more than half of Main Street, a forest fire and a psychopath trying to get away with murder," Ford said. "Battle Mountain—and everyone in it—is still here. What could a cartel do to us that we haven't already survived?"

Isla discarded her pastry, and Adan could've sworn hell had frozen over right then and there. She shoved to her feet, wiped sugar against her jeans and extended her uninjured hand. "Thanks, Chief. I won't let you down."

"I'd like it better if you'd give me a bite of your pastry to show your appreciation." Ford shook her hand.

Her laugh filled the room. "How about I bring you one tomorrow?"

"Deal." The chief nodded toward Adan. "Now get out of here. From the look on this guy's face, he's tired of talking."

Chief Ford had hit the mark.

"Call if you need something." Isla tossed the rest of her pastry in the garbage and reached for Adan.

He intertwined his hand with hers, and they made their way to the clinic parking lot. Swinging her into his chest, Adan held on to her as he sandwiched her between his body and her truck. "Congratulations.

You've still got a job. Ready to go grab Mazi from the ranch?"

The brightness in her gaze dimmed as she focused on something over his shoulder. "There's something I have to do first." She looked up at him. "Will you come with me?"

"Yeah." He released her, letting Isla take the lead.

She climbed behind the wheel, waited for him to buckle up and pulled out of the parking lot. Silence settled through the cab as they headed south. Back into the desert.

In less than fifteen minutes, she pulled the truck beside the house he would've been happy never to see again. Burgess's vehicle had been towed in as evidence. Nothing but dry, cracked desert to take in. Thrusting the vehicle into Park, she stared through the windshield, but didn't move. "Macie was able to go through the laundry list of corporations that own this place. Took a few days, but she finally found the original paperwork. Clint bought this place as part of his investigation into Fischer and his men, but the title belongs to you."

"What?" He scanned the landscape, focusing on the shattered front window, the hill where Isla had disappeared, the position the shooter had taken to the west. "Why?"

"I think he knew you'd pick up where he left off, and I think he wanted you to have a place to call home after Fischer and the rest of your unit were finally brought to justice." Confidence bled into her voice. "Do you want to go inside?"

His throat thickened with uncertainty. He nodded, pushing out of the truck, and headed for the front door. Isla took his hand before the old porch groaned under their combined weight, and they crossed the threshold together.

It looked the same inside. The old recliner, the stain on the floor where Layton Burgess had bled out. The overturned lamp. Home. "It's kind of a dump."

"Yeah, but you're good with your hands." She knocked their joined hands into the side of his thigh.

"What are you saying?" he asked.

"I'm saying, what if we made this our home?" She scanned the dilapidated kitchen with sagging cabinets and the bullet holes in the walls. "I know it's not much now, but it's something that's tied to us both. It'll take some time to get everything fixed up. On the upside there's plenty of room. Especially for a growing family."

A family? His heart shot into his throat. He'd never found himself worthy of the kind of life she and Clint had made together, but now…with the future ahead of them and Isla and Mazi at his side, Adan had never been more excited to start than right then. Her and Mazi's house was just that. A house, somewhere they'd restarted their lives. His safe house? Only tied to him. This place… It could be theirs. With some work. "It's perfect."

Her smile elicited the kind of heat meant to scar a man from the inside, and he couldn't get enough. Isla gasped as he dragged her into him. "I take it that's a yes?"

Adan kissed her with everything he had. "Can't wait to get started."

Epilogue

Macie Barclay was leaving Battle Mountain.

It didn't take a tarot reading or a lunar eclipse to tell her things were only going to get worse. Serial killers, bombers, psychopaths out for revenge, and now crimes connected to cartels? Nope. She was out of here just as soon as she'd packed everything. "Okay. What else?"

She shoved a few more dresses into her already bulging suitcase and went to the bathroom to see what she'd left behind. She wouldn't be able to take all her things, but she'd done this before. Keep what was important, leave the rest.

Too bad. She'd really loved this place. The entire house had been built around a one-hundred-year-old tree. Everyone in the department had joked about her tree house, but this had been the one house where she'd actually felt she belonged. Connected. Macie closed her eyes, taking in the feel of the cool breeze through the window, the smell of the wood that made up these walls. It had seemed perfect.

She'd make the next place perfect, too. No matter where that was.

Finished with packing her clothes and toiletries, she headed back to the closet tucked away in the loft she'd used as a bedroom for the past six years. Hangers slid out of her way easily as she reached for the bifold shutters she'd installed at the back.

Anyone who'd come through this place had questioned her taste in decor, especially inside a closet nobody would see, but she'd put them in for a reason. She tugged at the right and swung it wide. The photos and sticky notes she'd taped inside fluttered with the movement. Everything—crime scene photos she'd stolen from Albuquerque PD, the autopsy report filed by a corrupt medical examiner, notes of possible witnesses and family members to interview—it all had a place. Even one wrong placement could undo twenty years' worth of work.

Good thing she'd looked at this makeshift murder board a thousand times. She'd have no problem reassembling it wherever she ended up, but she unpocketed her phone and took a photo of the board as a whole just in case.

She peeled and untacked each piece of evidence she'd gathered since she was ten years old. No one would ever know why she'd joined Battle Mountain's police department. Or why she'd run from her hometown. And that was how it would have to stay. "There you go."

Macie tucked the slips of paper and photos and

reports into a file folder and slipped it into her messenger bag. This was it. She scanned the remains of the house. Everything she'd cared about was in that suitcase on the bed, but the people she'd gotten to know—the friends she'd made—they all had to stay here. Live their lives. Be happy. Find a way to survive.

She just couldn't do it with them anymore. It was too dangerous. Macie Barclay had been a good name while she'd been here, but that wasn't her anymore. She shouldered her bag and zipped the suitcase closed. She didn't know where she'd end up tonight. It didn't matter. As long as it wasn't here.

Her keys trilled in her hand as she hauled her suitcase off the bed and down the stairs. She'd done all the dishes, wiped down any surface that might hold her fingerprints and cleaned out the refrigerator. If anyone came looking for her, they wouldn't have the slightest idea of where to start, and her heart hurt at the idea Chief Ford, Cree, Alma, hell, even Easton, had never really gotten the chance to know the real her. Never would. That was just how it needed to be.

She gazed up into the exposed rafters and set her hand against the thickest part of the tree climbing up through the roof. "You were exactly what I needed when I needed it. Thank you. For everything."

Macie gripped the handle of her suitcase with one hand and her shoulder strap with the other. "Time to go."

She swung the front door open. And froze.

A man had raised his fist to knock, and a tendril of fear slithered through her. He was handsome, devastatingly so, with piercing blue eyes that widened at the sight of her, but she'd been fooled by good looks before. And somehow, she knew him. Like they'd met before. "Macie Barclay?"

"Sorry. She doesn't live here anymore." She had to get out of here. "Wish I could help, but I'm running late for my flight. If you'll excuse me." Macie managed to get past him and closed the front door behind her. She was halfway down the curving stairs before he tried again.

"Ava?" he asked.

She almost let go of her suitcase at the name. No one had called her that since she'd been a girl running around with braids in her hair and as much sugar as she could haul in her pockets back in Albuquerque. Macie forced herself to keep moving. To get away. Nobody was supposed to find her here. She'd been careful. What had she done wrong? "Sorry. I don't know anyone by that name. I hope you find what you're looking for."

"It's me. Riggs." He took a step down. Then another. "Riggs Karig. Do you remember me?"

Air crushed from her chest. She looked up at him from the bottom of the staircase. It hadn't been her imagination. The eyes, the shape of his mouth, the note of concern in his voice. For a moment, she saw her childhood best friend as the boy he'd been in the man he'd become, and her plan faded to the back of her mind.

Riggs.

He took another step down. A flash of a badge peeked out from beneath his jacket, and in an instant, the memories were gone. All that was left was regret she hadn't packed faster. She snuck her hand toward the pocket on the outside of her messenger bag where she'd kept a can of pepper spray the minute she'd arrived in Battle Mountain. "I told you, you have the wrong woman."

Macie forced herself to keep moving toward her crappy four-door sedan. She tossed her suitcase into the back seat and climbed behind the steering wheel.

Then suddenly Riggs was there. He was holding her door open, but she started the car anyway. "Avalynn, please. I need your help."

He was the only one who could get away with calling her by her full name. Macie gripped the steering wheel, knowing she'd regret not closing the door on his hand and making a break for it. She'd never been able to resist his charm in the past. Why would twenty years change anything? She forced herself to take a deep breath. "Help you with what?"

Riggs dug for a piece of paper in his jacket and handed it to her. "You can start by explaining why my friend was found dead with your name and address in his pocket."

* * * * *

Get 4 FREE REWARDS!

We'll send you 2 FREE Books plus 2 FREE Mystery Gifts.

FREE Value Over **$20**

Both the **Harlequin Intrigue®** and **Harlequin® Romantic Suspense** series feature compelling novels filled with heart-racing action-packed romance that will keep you on the edge of your seat.

YES! Please send me 2 FREE novels from the Harlequin Intrigue or Harlequin Romantic Suspense series and my 2 FREE gifts (gifts are worth about $10 retail). After receiving them, if I don't wish to receive any more books, I can return the shipping statement marked "cancel." If I don't cancel, I will receive 6 brand-new Harlequin Intrigue Larger-Print books every month and be billed just $6.49 each in the U.S. or $6.99 each in Canada, a savings of at least 13% off the cover price, or 4 brand-new Harlequin Romantic Suspense books every month and be billed just $5.49 each in the U.S. or $6.24 each in Canada, a savings of at least 12% off the cover price. It's quite a bargain! Shipping and handling is just 50¢ per book in the U.S. and $1.25 per book in Canada.* I understand that accepting the 2 free books and gifts places me under no obligation to buy anything. I can always return a shipment and cancel at any time by calling the number below. The free books and gifts are mine to keep no matter what I decide.

Choose one: ☐ **Harlequin Intrigue Larger-Print** (199/399 HDN GRJK) ☐ **Harlequin Romantic Suspense** (240/340 HDN GRJK)

Name (please print)

Address   Apt. #

City   State/Province   Zip/Postal Code

Email: Please check this box ☐ if you would like to receive newsletters and promotional emails from Harlequin Enterprises ULC and its affiliates. You can unsubscribe anytime.

Mail to the **Harlequin Reader Service:**
IN U.S.A.: P.O. Box 1341, Buffalo, NY 14240-8531
IN CANADA: P.O. Box 603, Fort Erie, Ontario L2A 5X3

Want to try 2 free books from another series! Call 1-800-873-8635 or visit www.ReaderService.com.

*Terms and prices subject to change without notice. Prices do not include sales taxes, which will be charged (if applicable) based on your state or country of residence. Canadian residents will be charged applicable taxes. Offer not valid in Quebec. This offer is limited to one order per household. Books received may not be as shown. Not valid for current subscribers to the Harlequin Intrigue or Harlequin Romantic Suspense series. All orders subject to approval. Credit or debit balances in a customer's account(s) may be offset by any other outstanding balance owed by or to the customer. Please allow 4 to 6 weeks for delivery. Offer available while quantities last.

Your Privacy—Your information is being collected by Harlequin Enterprises ULC, operating as Harlequin Reader Service. For a complete summary of the information we collect, how we use this information and to whom it is disclosed, please visit our privacy notice located at corporate.harlequin.com/privacy-notice. From time to time we may also exchange your personal information with reputable third parties. If you wish to opt out of this sharing of your personal information, please visit readerservice.com/consumerschoice or call 1-800-873-8635. **Notice to California Residents**—Under California law, you have specific rights to control and access your data. For more information on these rights and how to exercise them, visit corporate.harlequin.com/california-privacy.

HIHRS22R3

HARLEQUIN
PLUS

Try the best multimedia
subscription service for romance
readers like you!

Read, Watch and Play.

Experience the easiest way to get
the romance content you crave.

Start your **FREE TRIAL** at
<u>www.harlequinplus.com/freetrial</u>.